In loving memory of
Myrtle "Nannie" Morris

Awaken the Dead

Holly Copella

ACKNOWLEDGMENTS

Copella Books: First Paperback Edition 2016
Printed by CreateSpace, An Amazon.com Company
Cover Artist: Daniela Owergoor
Dani-owergoor.deviantart.com

PUBLISHER'S NOTE

This is a work of fiction. Names, character, places, and incidents either are the product of the author's imagination or are used fictitiously, and any resemblance to actual persons, living or dead, business establishments, events or locales is entirely coincidental. The publisher does not have any control over and does not assume any responsibility for author or third-party Web sites or their content.

Chapter One

The majestic Horizon Hotel was situated on the massive cliff overlooking the ocean as a fierce storm rolled inland. The century old, gray stone hotel was moderately dark with few lights on inside, indicating the power had gone out, as it tended to during storms. The backup generator was undoubtedly running, providing only emergency lighting and some additional comforts for hotel guests. The wind blew while the rain continued to pour down and lightning lit up the dark, night sky. The old, well-kept red and white lighthouse was nestled alongside the hotel with its impressive light calling to passing ships. Historically, it was a lifesaving beacon on stormy nights, making ships aware of the jagged rocks just offshore. With modern technology, most vessels had their own guidance systems, making lighthouses more iconic than functional except in cases of smaller, personal boats.

A well-maintained set of iron steps led down the massive cliff to the private, secluded beach below. The beach was inaccessible except by the steps built into the cliff or by boat. Jagged rocks both east and west kept the beach completely private. On that particular night, the surf was rough, crashing to shore with a vengeance. As the thunder clashed and lightning lit up the dark night sky, a woman was heard screaming. Someone plummeted from the hotel's third story balcony on the cliff down to the jagged rocks near the beach below.

✝

*O*ne year later. The Horizon Hotel's impressive lobby was rustic with natural, handcrafted woodwork throughout. The cathedral ceiling contained thick tree trunks used as support beams, adding to the rustic appeal. The second floor contained a balcony, which was open to the lobby below. The lobby floor was created from natural bluestone, although many area rugs were scattered about. The furniture was as rustic as the lobby itself, also handcrafted from actual trees. The large coffee table made from a slice of tree trunk, which still contained the bark, was one of many showpieces within the lobby. The front desk was hand carved from wood and painstakingly detailed with depictions of wildlife. The rustic details of the lodge remained intact from the time the hotel was first built by its original owners a century ago. Three salty seamen had fallen into a sizeable fortune and had chosen the remote lighthouse property for their secluded hotel venture.

Early that evening, a young woman in her mid-twenties sat behind the front desk with a book in her hand, remaining completely engrossed in her novel. Remy Townshend was a natural beauty with shoulder length, silky black hair, which she wore pulled back into a neatly kempt ponytail. She wore little make-up as her naturally bronzed skin was flawless and her dark lashes gave the impression of eyeliner. Her athletic build and girl next-door appeal made her look right at home in the impressive lobby. The lobby was deathly quiet, as it was most days and nights during the off-season. A shelf full of books was the only thing that kept the young woman from slipping into a comatose state.

Another woman in her early twenties, Harley Brandon, approached the front desk while clutching her electronic tablet. Harley had flowing golden-brown hair, which she wore slightly longer, allowing it to fall free several inches past her shoulders. She was equally attractive as her friend behind the desk but with a different sort of appeal. Daintier than her friend, Harley was moderately feminine in comparison. She wore eyeliner to accent her eyelashes and a reddish brown lipstick brought out her lips. Not nearly as athletic as Remy, Harley maintained a slim waist, ample breasts, and a shapely posterior. Running around the hotel throughout the day was enough to keep both women in fairly decent shape without half trying.

With rising frustration, Harley frantically tapped on the tablet she held in her hand. She cursed softly with each tap to the screen. She paused before Remy at the desk, although her presence didn't garner a response. Harley was too busy beating the tablet screen to note her friend's indifferent mood.

"Do you have any idea what's wrong with this stupid thing?" Harley asked and continued to strike the tablet. "It just keeps blinking at me."

Remy didn't look up, offered no comment, and refused to acknowledge her. Harley looked at the woman engrossed in her book and the cold reception she'd been given. Remy was her best friend but also her employee, further exasperating the situation. Remy worked for her room, board, and some pocket change. It wasn't ideal, but it was the best Harley could offer at the moment, forcing her friend to keep her weekend evening job at the local tavern. The hotel was running on some hard times and it had taken its toll on all of them. Harley studied Remy and frowned at her lack of acknowledgment.

"Are you still mad at me because I needed you to work tonight?" Harley questioned.

It had been her friend's only night off, but Harley was in a bind and needed her, particularly since they actually had guests that weekend. Remy continued to ignore her. Harley felt her frustration rising, but she wasn't going to let Remy's silent tantrum ruffle her. Good *cheap* help was hard to find in the remote, summer town. She groaned softy with defeat and attempted to keep from lashing out at her friend, for the sake of their friendship.

"Fine, I'll ask Murdock to look at it," Harley muttered with some disgust in her tone.

As Harley turned and left the desk, Remy finally looked up from her book. She stared across the lobby only a moment, shook her head with little emotion, and then returned to her book as if she wasn't the least bit interested in what had just happened.

Chapter Two

*H*arley crossed the lobby after her less than warming welcome from her friend overseeing the front desk. She continued to struggle with her handheld device, which was getting the better of her at the moment. She saw something out of the corner of her eye and immediately lifted her head. Whatever she thought she had seen wasn't there. She shivered slightly despite the warmth of the lobby. It wasn't the first time Harley had seen or heard things she couldn't explain. She made no secret that she thought the hotel was haunted. Her parents and her friends all thought she was certifiable, but she knew what she saw and felt. On several occasions, she'd sworn she felt a cold hand touching her. Naturally, there was nothing there, but she knew she wasn't crazy.

Lately, though, her unexplained paranormal episodes seemed to escalate. She was starting to see disturbing images that she hadn't before. Most times, it was just a brief flash, but they were typically enough to cause severe tension. She nearly stepped in a large bloodstain on the stone floor toward the center of the lobby. She

6

took a quick step back and stared at the bloodstain, but just that fast, it was gone. The recent uptick in paranormal activity was unnerving and at times made her look flighty in front of others. Harley often avoided stepping on certain areas of floor or suddenly stopped to avoid stepping in imaginary blood.

She finally let the image on the floor slip from her mind, returning her attention to her tablet and again pounded on it as she headed toward the elevators. Harley nearly collided with a lanky man in his late twenties. She was slightly rattled by his sudden appearance, particularly after what she had once again witnessed on the floor. Although not a handsome man, Murdock Martin had a certain comedic appeal. His sandy brown hair was styled business short. His light blue eyes were oddly trusting yet his moderately crooked smile conveyed his lack of seriousness.

"Are you still fighting with that thing?" Murdock asked, not the least bit concerned about nearly colliding with her.

"When it comes to electronics, I swear I'm cursed," she muttered.

"Did you ask Remy?" Murdock enquired with a curious, although less than serious look. "You know she's great with electronics."

Harley groaned softly and hid her frown while gently indicating the woman behind the desk. "She's still mad at me about having to work tonight."

He shook his head in response while expressing his annoyance. "What's with her lately?" Murdock demanded. "She's been acting all huffy with me too."

Both watched Remy round the desk and head toward the main corridor, disappearing from their sight.

Murdock returned his attention to Harley as his brows raised. "You're the mean boss making her work late," he remarked. "She shouldn't take it out on me. I mean, really, you're making me work late too."

Harley glared at him and showed little emotion. "Murdock, you don't work here," she firmly reminded him.

He stared at her with a look of surprise and blinked several times with a childlike innocence. "Then why was I unclogging toilets this afternoon?"

"I wonder the same thing myself," she teased and offered a smile.

He casually cocked his head to the side, folded his arms across his chest, and glared at her. "With that attitude, it's no wonder Remy's mad at you."

"You know I appreciate everything you do around here, Murdock," she began gently, "but I hate that you do so much without being paid."

"I know you've been struggling to keep the hotel from sinking since the death of your parents," he replied firmly. "I'm not going to let you struggle alone. Besides, you let me live here rent free."

"Rent free," she scoffed and had to keep from laughing. "That's a good one. If it wasn't for all the groceries you buy, I'd probably starve to death."

"See, another reason you need me to help out."

Harley stared at him almost at a loss for words. He wasn't bragging; he did so much for her. She was lost somewhere between grateful and helpless. "I don't know what I'd do without you, Murdock. I mean that."

"Well, if you ever feel like repaying me--"

"Don't start with that," she announced, cutting him off. Her gratitude only went so far. "Our relationship is perfect the way it is. You're my best friend. I don't want to ruin that by us dating. You know it won't work." She hesitated and frowned before allowing the words to spill from her mouth. "You know I'd make a lousy girlfriend."

"How would you know?" he countered while studying her. "You never tried being one."

She didn't want to get into another debate about her lack of a love life. It had been a trying night as it was. "Isn't there a clogged toilet calling you?"

"No, but with seven guests, I'm sure there's something I should be doing," he replied cheerfully. "Early spring and we have six rooms booked. Might be a good sign to the start of the summer season."

"We're not even half booked yet for the summer," she reminded him with defeat. "I don't even know if we have enough guests coming this summer to survive the season."

"You'll book a few more rooms. Remy's been working on updating the website," he reminded her while keeping an upbeat attitude. "It'll work out. I should probably check on the frat boys and their muse." He then frowned and shook his head. "I can't believe the new guest hasn't complained about their late night parties."

"Remy put the new guest in a room at the opposite end of the hotel," she remarked then groaned softly as she shook her head.

"I wish the Gooding's would let me move them to another area of the hotel as well."

"No, they'd rather complain," Murdock replied. "I think they're looking for a discount on their stay."

"I gave Kaplan his ocean view suite at regular room rate," she announced. "I think that's more than generous."

Two men in their late twenties approached from the main corridor just beyond the elevators. Rhodes and Decker were part of the guests Harley and Murdock fondly referred to as 'the frat party'. Their group consisted of three men and one woman, all of whom had been staying at the hotel for longer than Harley could remember. Rhodes was a tall, slightly muscular man with flowing black hair. Although he was handsome by almost any standard, his personality and temperament were enough to kill any fantasy involving him. He almost certainly had an ego to match. He dressed biker casual with torn jeans and an excessively tight tee shirt to show off his muscular arms.

His counterpart, Decker, had an ego nearly as big as his burly friend. He was less attractive than Rhodes was and not nearly as impressive in height or build. Decker had slightly longer, light brown hair that nearly touched his shoulders. He dressed with a preppy sort of appeal opposite Rhodes' bad boy look.

Harley made a face the moment she saw the men. "Oh, great," she groaned softly. "I can't deal with Rhodes. He gives me some serious creeps." She cast a glance at Murdock, feeling bad for pawning them off on him. "Will you handle whatever their problem is tonight?"

"I'm at your service," Murdock teased while flashing a smile. "Go on. Take off."

Harley patted his arm while grinning then hurried across the lobby in the opposite direction. She carefully rounded the spot she had earlier imagined the bloodstain and left through the beachside terrace doors. Murdock casually approached the front desk and walked behind it, pretending to be busy. Rhodes and Decker paused within the lobby and stared after Harley, who had vanished through the terrace doors. Their expressions were an odd sort of disappointment. Decker frowned and turned toward his friend while secretly nodding in the direction of the front desk.

"I thought you said the lapdog was going out tonight," Decker muttered with some irritation.

"I guess he changed his mind," Rhodes snarled back.

"So now what?"

"We continue with the original plan," Rhodes announced firmly. "You send the lapdog outside to chase his tail around for a while."

"What about the girl?" Decker suddenly protested. "She could come back inside any minute."

"Doubtful," he replied. "She spends hours in that old lighthouse for some strange reason. I only need fifteen minutes to search the office." Rhodes' look turned demanding. "Certainly you can get rid of Murdock for fifteen minutes."

"Yeah, sure," Decker replied. "I'll come up with something."

Rhodes nodded then headed back down the hall and paused before the elevator, although he didn't press the button. Decker approached Murdock behind the desk. Murdock looked up from the computer and put on his best faux smile.

"Good evening, Decker," Murdock announced almost too cheerfully. "What can I do for you?"

"I don't want to alarm you," Decker began while forcing a concerned look, "but I think I saw some kids on the private beach below the cliff. Seemed to be making quite a mess. Wouldn't doubt they're drinking. You know, I found some glass bottles on the beach this morning."

"Oh, great," Murdock groaned. "That's all I need. Excuse me."

Murdock headed out from behind the desk and hurried for the beachside terrace doors. Decker watched Murdock hurrying across the terrace then smiled and signaled to Rhodes. Rhodes hurried down the hall, paused before the office door, and worked on the lock. Within a few seconds, he sprung the lock and hurried into the dark office.

The hotel office was mostly organized, although the large desktop was moderately cluttered with papers and junk that spilled out onto the floor. The furniture was functional and not nearly as awe-inspiring as the rest of the hotel. Harley kept the office as her father had left it. The office contained far too many boat related decorations nailed to the walls or sitting on shelves for Harley's taste. Rhodes quickly searched the desk drawers and routed through several cabinets. After a few minutes, he became disgusted and looked around. His eyes fell upon the old secretary hutch on the opposite side of the office. He approached the old desk and searched through the drawers. Rhodes eyes suddenly lit up.

"There you are," he announced softly and chuckled.

He removed a small stack of folded blueprints. Without even looking at them, he removed the entire bunch and hurried for the door. He shut off the light and closed the door behind him.

Chapter Three

*T*he sun was setting over the horizon, giving the ocean a brilliant yet tranquil, glassy appeal. It was low tide and the surf gently lapped to shore. The lighthouse continued to send signals to distant boats. The beacon was an impressive view from the secluded beach below. At the end of the beach was the private boat dock then the steep, iron steps leading back up to the lighthouse and hotel. Within the impressive lighthouse, Harley sat in the lantern room on a comfortable, padded bench facing the ocean. She stared out at the ocean for several minutes or perhaps a lifetime. She'd spent much of her free time in the lantern room just keeping watch. Sometimes she'd pace the widow's walk, but only during warmer days. She drifted back into her own thoughts.

One year earlier. Harley walked along the wooden dock attached to the beach just at the base of the cliffs. At the end of the dock was the most impressive vintage yacht anyone had ever seen. The yacht resembled something out of an old pirate movie. It was in immaculate condition and the mere sight of it was enough to give Harley goosebumps. There was no doubt her father made the right choice by buying the yacht. Now her father was about to take *The*

Dream Catcher out for a daytrip. Rollin, or Skipper as he preferred to be called while playing with his new toy, finished loading his fishing gear onto the deck of the impressive yacht. Harley approached and stood near the gangplank. She grinned while watching her father's childlike fascination for *The Dream Catcher's* maiden voyage under his command.

"Permission to come aboard, Skipper?" she announced with equal enthusiasm.

Her father straightened, looked back at her, and grinned while tilting his white skipper's hat back on his full head of dark hair. Rollin was a ruggedly handsome gentleman in his late forties and stood roughly 5'11", although he made a big deal out of stretching his height to a respectable six feet tall. He was more athletic than muscular, although he'd gotten a little out of shape the last few years, possibly since Harley had been away at college. She couldn't confirm it, but Harley suspected her parents had been dining out more often with her away at school. The refrigerator tended to be a little empty on her return visits.

"Permission granted," he cheerfully announced.

Harley walked the short gangplank and joined her father on deck. He seemed a little too cheerful while grinning at her. He was always like a kid in a candy store when it came to new boats or anything boat related.

"Have you changed your mind about joining us?" he questioned.

Although Harley wanted to play with her father's new ship, the daytrip sounded like a romantic 'couple's only' sort of thing. She'd have plenty of time to enjoy outings on the yacht. It seemed more important to allow her parents their romantic day alone together. She knew her father would thank her for her thoughtfulness later.

"No, I was just coming to witness the launching of your old girl," Harley announced.

"Now, Harley," he scolded. "That's hardly a nice thing to say about your mother."

She hid her smile at his tasteless joke. A casually dressed woman in her late forties stood behind Rollin with her arms folded across her chest and a sneer on her moderately youthful looking face. She smacked Rollin on the upper arm, the loud crack startling him more than the actual slap. He laughed and looked back at Harley's mother. Rita wasn't impressed with her husband's idea of a joke at her expense.

"I knew you were standing there," he teased.

Despite being in her late forties, her mother looked much younger than her actual age. She had always had a youthful appearance. A few new wrinkles had appeared around her mother's eyes since Harley returned from college. She often wondered if her mother had trouble sleeping again. When Harley first left for college, Murdock would report that her mother seemed tired all the time. Rita had terrible bouts with insomnia. Despite that Harley never had trouble sleeping, women in her family tended to fall victim to sleeplessness. Rita kept her golden-brown hair at shoulder length. Apart from a small patch of gray near her temple, Rita was mostly free from gray hair. Rita and Harley looked similar in appearance, easily indicating they were related. Some had actually mistaken Harley's mother for an older sister. Rita shifted her attention to Harley and offered a warm, pleasant smile.

"If you're sure you won't join us," Rita announced cheerfully to her daughter, "there's some money on the counter for dinner tonight."

Harley groaned softly and had to keep from laughing. "I don't need you leaving money for dinner, Mom."

"I'm pretty sure the cupboards are bare," Rita informed her then hid her smile and shook her head. "Murdock's been eating us out of house and home."

"Honestly," Rollin muttered, "I don't know where that boy puts it. He's as skinny as a rail."

"Just take the money," Rita replied cheerfully then looked to the sunny sky. "We'll be back before dark."

"I hope so," Harley announced. "You know they're calling for bad weather this evening."

"That's not coming until late tonight," Rollin replied then hugged Harley. "You behave while we're gone. Keep Murdock out of trouble."

"The hotel is a ghost town," Harley informed him. "There's no trouble to be had."

Rollin suddenly groaned. "Don't use the 'g' word," he muttered. "If word of hauntings gets around, we'll be selling tours as a top ten most haunted places."

"Don't worry, Dad," Harley replied. "I haven't seen or heard anything strange since I've been home. I think your kindred spirits moved on."

A few minutes later, Harley was back on the dock waving to her parents as *The Dream Catcher* sailed away like a ghostly apparition. As Harley watched the ship until it was nearly out of sight, a chill swept over her. She clutched her chilled arms and shivered slightly.

Present day. Harley remained sitting on the bench within the lighthouse lantern room and stared at the darkening horizon. She clutched her chilled shoulders and silently watched nothing in particular. She never felt more sad and alone.

Chapter Four

$\mathcal{J}$ust after dark that evening, the front lobby doors opened to reveal a neatly dressed man in his mid-thirties with an attractive woman clinging to his arm. Alicia Lang giggled while leaning on Dane as they entered. Alicia had long, golden blond hair, flawless make-up, and a nearly perfect body to match. Her clothes were moderately expensive for someone born and raised in the small resort town. Being the town's only realtor, she was required to look the part of a sophisticated woman. Alicia was almost certainly high maintenance, although it appeared as if Dane could afford her. Dane Wright was a fairly handsome man, although not necessarily in Alicia's league. His clothes, despite being business casual, screamed wealth, which helped explain Alicia's attraction. His brown hair was kept neatly trimmed, although slightly longer than what would be considered a buzz cut. He wore a button shirt with a casual jacket by a name brand designer, indicating he definitely wasn't local.

Alicia leaned on his shoulder and seemed reluctant to release his arm. "Are you sure you had fun tonight?"

"When you said 'barn dance', I didn't think you actually meant it'd be in a barn," he teased while grinning, "but, yes, I had fun. Although next time, I'll dress down for the occasion."

"You made quite the impression on the locals," she announced cheerfully. "I felt like queen of the barn dance with you by my side."

He chuckled softly and appeared almost embarrassed. "You only mentioned my jewelry store forty times," he replied.

"Our little town never had a real jewelry store before. I'm just trying to get your name out there," Alicia announced with enthusiasm. "I'm in real estate. Word of mouth means everything in my business. Besides, if you're going to afford that million-dollar estate you made an offer on, you'll need the business."

"I wouldn't worry too much, Alicia," he informed her. "I have clients all over the city willing to drive to the country for my creations."

"That's so exciting. I can't believe I'm dating the rock star of rocks."

He allowed a throaty chuckle to escape. "You just love saying that, don't you?"

"Most exciting two weeks of my life," she replied then turned up the charm. "How about some wine in the terrace hot tub?"

"Anything you want," Dane announced while grinning. "Why don't you go to the room and change while I see about scoring a bottle of wine from the desk clerk?"

"Don't be long."

She kissed him quickly on the lips then headed for the elevators. Dane grinned while watching her leave. It was difficult not to admire her backside in her form-fitting dress. Dane finally turned and headed for the front desk. Remy immediately set her book down and smiled pleasantly.

"Good evening, Mr. Wright," Remy announced.

"Please, call me Dane. I hate formalities," he replied then appeared curious. "Is there somewhere I can get a bottle of wine this time of night?"

"In this town?" she teased then laughed. "Unlikely. But if you don't tell the liquor control board, the wine cellar is still stocked. Technically I'm not allowed to sell you any liquor, but if you don't tell, I won't."

"It'll be our little secret."

"Wait here, I'll find a bottle for you," she announced while springing up from her tall chair. "White or red?"

"Either is fine, thanks."

The lights flickered and then came back a little less bright then they had been. Dane and Remy both glanced at the dim lights. He appeared more curious, while Remy seemed slightly tense. There was an odd silence between them. When he noted her mood change, Dane attempted a smile.

"Power lines must be bad on top of your little hill," Dane remarked.

Remy held her shoulders and suddenly shivered. She attempted to cover with a smile. "Yeah, they do that a lot at night," Remy replied, although she didn't sound convincing. She managed an uneasy laugh. "Some claim the hotel is haunted."

"I'm guessing you share the sediment," he teased.

She forced a tiny shrug and attempted to release her chilled arms, but she found it difficult. "A little silly to believe in ghosts, don't you think?"

"Oh, I don't know," he replied. "I'm inclined to keep an open mind. This place has some serious creep appeal in the evening."

"I think that has more to do with the dark wood throughout than actual paranormal activity," Remy remarked then fidgeted. "Although, there have been a few chilling deaths over the hotel's one hundred year history."

"Really?" he replied almost too quickly then hid his enthusiasm with a smile. "God, I can be such a research geek. Folklore and superstitions fascinate me."

"Well, if you want to read up on the history of our little town and the hotel, there's a book on the coffee table near the fireplace," she informed him. "I've personally heard enough of the tales from town gossips over the years."

Dane attempted to hide his enthusiastic smile. "I'll just pretend I'm not a nerd and collect that book after you've gone."

Remy managed an uneasy laugh, inhaled deeply, and attempted a smile, although she suddenly seemed uncomfortable. "I'll get that wine for you."

Remy hurried from behind the desk and headed down the corridor past the elevators. Dane leaned on the front desk and glanced over the book Remy had been reading. It was a gory horror story. Dane grimaced at the grisly cover. He hesitated then picked up the book and read the first page. The terrace door was heard opening, and a cool breeze blew across the lobby. Dane instinctively looked toward the terrace doors. Harley walked across the lobby with a handful of flowers. Dane watched her with great interest and possible surprise to her presence.

Harley placed the flowers in a vase on the library table with other flowers and casually arranged them. She looked across the lobby and saw Dane staring at her. He stared at her longer than he should have and appeared unable to look away. Harley took a moment to admire the well-dressed man, smiled, and approached him at the desk. Dane uncertainly turned as she approached and returned his attention to Remy's book, as if pretending he hadn't been looking at her. Harley paused alongside him and admired his profile. Despite the ten-year age difference, she found the man attractive in a distinguished sort of way. He avoided looking at her, which she found slightly odd. Perhaps he didn't want her to think he'd been staring, even though she'd clearly caught him in the act. Being outgoing was her new lot in life since she took over responsibility for the hotel. It wasn't something she was comfortable doing, but she knew it fell upon her to initiate conversations with strangers.

"I'm sorry I didn't get a chance to greet you when you arrived this afternoon," Harley announced cheerfully to the distinguished man.

Dane tensed while staring at the book cover then uncertainly cast a look at Harley. He stared at her a moment as his lips parted and appeared uncertain how to respond.

"I'm, uh, sorry," he fumbled slightly and attempted a smile. "Were you talking to me?"

Harley grinned and held back her laugh. Was it possible he'd actually been checking her out rather than just casually looking? He was certainly acting guilty of something. Considering the current company he was keeping, Harley found it difficult to believe she would catch the attention of any man who already had someone like Alicia on the hook.

"There's no one else here," she teased then extended her hand. "I'm Harley Brandon, the hotel owner."

Dane stared at her hand a moment then met her gaze with a strange look. She looked at her hand, smiled with embarrassment at the dirt on her fingers, and wiped them on her pants.

"Sorry. I was out picking flowers," she informed him. "I forget not everyone likes a little good, clean dirt." She straightened proudly and studied him. "You're Dane Wright, right?"

Harley grinned at her own joke even if Dane didn't seem amused by it. Dane continued to stare then managed a smile, almost as if suddenly getting her play on words.

"Yes, I'm Dane," he replied and stared at her with a strange fascination. "*You're* Harley Brandon? The hotel owner?"

"You seem surprised," she announced then grinned. "I know I'm rather young to be running my own hotel. I get that a lot." She fidgeted slightly. "My parents died last year, so I've been trying to carry the torch. This hotel has been in the family since it was built over one hundred years ago."

"It's, uh, impressive."

"It needs work, I know," she replied, almost certain he'd been thinking it. "The tourist season last summer hadn't been that good. We're getting by until the renovation loan is approved." Harley swiftly changed the subject to something less depressing. "I heard you rented a shop in town. Diamonds, I recall."

He fidgeted then smiled. "Yes."

"Not exactly the wealthiest town," she replied then casually shrugged. "Summer might prove lucrative with all the tourists flooding our town, but you may starve over the winter."

"I'll gladly sacrifice the revenue for the peace and quiet," he informed her.

"Won't get much of that around here either," Harley announced and withheld her laugh. "This town is full of gossip girls. Of course, I'm sure Alicia warned you already."

"Actually, she hadn't mentioned it."

"I'm surprised she hadn't mentioned her newly found relationship either. I had to hear about it through the Remy grapevine," she replied.

"Well," he announced delicately, "Alicia and I just started dating a week ago, so she may have been reluctant to mention it."

"Oh, only a week?" Harley recapped then realized how it must have sounded. She quickly covered. "How did you two meet?"

"Uh, well, we met two weeks ago when Alicia was showing me homes in town," he informed her and seemed to relax slightly. "After all that time together looking at homes, I suppose it was only natural that we'd start seeing each other socially."

Harley smiled in response, but she couldn't help noting his wishy-washy comment to his relationship. Perhaps he wasn't so much interested in a relationship as he was a fling with his flirty real estate agent. He didn't seem to have that 'rich boy' ego, but she could be wrong.

"My brownstone in the city sold faster than I'd anticipated," he continued, "so I'm stuck living out of my suitcase until I close on a house here."

She held back her grin. "Are you buying the Foster Estate?"

"Well, waiting for a response on my offer," he replied with some surprise then appeared curious. "How did you know I was buying that place?"

"I know this town and I know the people in it," she informed him. "Alicia loves that house. She's been trying to sell it for quite some time. A successful businessman wearing an Armani jacket--?" She chuckled softly in her throat. "Yeah, she's selling you the Foster Estate."

"You certainly have a good read on people."

"One of my many useless talents," she teased. "I can read people, but I can't figure them out to save my life."

Remy approached with a bottle of wine. Harley groaned softly then smiled at Dane.

"I'm assuming Remy is about to do something I shouldn't know about," she teased, although she actually didn't want to get into a fight with her friend tonight, so it was best to just avoid her for now. "I'll let you get back to your evening. Goodnight."

He smiled more naturally. "Goodnight, Harley."

Harley walked across the lobby to avoid Remy. Dane watched her leave with a curious stare, giving her his undivided attention. She sidestepped around the area in which she'd earlier seen the bloodstain and continued on her way. Dane appeared curious, tilted his head, and then uncertainly crossed the lobby in the direction Harley had headed. He paused by the area of floor she had purposely stepped around and studied the stone. He slowly circled the area while staring with great interest. Remy approached with the bottle of wine in the crook of her arm and paused just a few feet away to watch him. Her look was odd and almost concerned.

"Something of interest?" she asked with a slight crackle in her voice.

Dane glanced at her but remained focused on the area of floor. He managed a tiny smile. "The, uh, stone here seems a shade off from the rest of the surrounding floor."

"You're certainly observant," Remy remarked while attempting to relax. "Undoubtedly a spill of some sort. It's been like that forever."

Dane stared at the area a moment longer, twitched slightly, then looked at Remy and managed a smile. "Yes, stone can be unforgiving when it comes to stains."

She handed him the bottle of wine while forcing a smile. He accepted the bottle and noted her look. Remy knew something she wasn't sharing; something she found deeply disturbing.

"I'll be at the desk for another hour," she informed him. "If you need anything after that, just dial the desk from your room phone. All calls will come to me in my room."

"I'm sure I won't need anything else tonight," he announced and offered a sincere smile while indicating the bottle. "Thanks for the wine."

"Sure," Remy replied more naturally. "You have a good night."

Remy headed back for the front desk then hesitated and glanced over her shoulder. Dane continued to study the area of stone floor. Remy rubbed her chilled arms and headed behind the desk.

Chapter Five

*T*he small terrace was located along the beachside of the hotel between the hotel lobby and the cliffs, giving an awe-inspiring view particularly during sunrise and sunset. The terrace contained the in-ground pool, which remained covered for the off-season. Alongside the pool was a large, sunken hot tub with a breathtaking view for a romantic experience. The evening was blissfully peaceful. Dane and Alicia cuddled within the back corner of the hot tub facing the ocean. They sipped wine and stole an occasional kiss. A couple in their late twenties, the remaining two members of 'the frat party', had joined Dane and Alicia in their once romantic hot tub for two. Patrice and Blaine groped and kissed passionately to the point of obscene, although Dane and Alicia appeared unaffected by their behavior. Patrice was a slender woman with excessively large breasts attempting to free themselves from her skimpy bikini top. Her long curly hair was unnaturally red, although not nearly as red as a clown's hair. She wore excessive eyeliner and make-up, adding to her prostitute-like appeal.

Blaine was average in just about every aspect from his height to his weight and build. He wore his brown hair business short and, despite spending most of his time drunk while at the hotel, he managed to remain clean-shaven. He was neither handsome nor unappealing. Alongside Patrice, he seemed dull in comparison, suggesting he was unequipped to handle the sexually energetic woman. She clearly dominated him in their hot tub adventure, although neither seemed to care about their behavior in front of the other guests.

Alicia affectionately clung to Dane's arm while cuddling against him and smiled lustfully. "I'm glad you asked me to stay the weekend with you," she cooed seductively.

He withheld his chuckle as he eyed her. "I'm still surprised you agreed."

"Why?" she asked while giggling. "Do you think small town girls are all virgins?"

"I wouldn't go that far, but I fear for your reputation," he remarked. "Everyone seems to know everyone's business in this town, or so I've been told, and we've only been out on a couple of official dates." He gave her a teasing smile. "What will people think?"

"That I found the perfect man," she cooed while clinging to his shoulder. "Is that why you didn't want to stay at my place until you closed on your house?"

"If they even accept the offer, it could take a month to close, and you live with your sister and her husband," he reminded her. "I just thought this would be best."

"I can't argue with you on that."

Patrice groaned softly, now straddling Blaine in the hot tub just a few feet away from Dane and Alicia. Both easily ignored the lustful couple.

Alicia nuzzled Dane, apparently feeling frisky herself. "At least here, we practically have the entire hotel to ourselves," she whispered seductively.

Dane instinctively looked across the terrace, frowned, and suddenly appeared distracted. He fidgeted slightly. "Not entirely to ourselves."

Murdock crossed the terrace with purpose and a look of irritation as he approached the hot tub. Dane silently watched him approach the opposite corner of the tub containing the overly affectionate couple.

Murdock crouched near Patrice and Blaine with a hardened look on his usually docile face. "Excuse me--"

They continued to kiss, grope, and grind against each other as their moans grew louder.

"Excuse me," Murdock snarled in a more demanding tone.

Patrice moved off Blaine and adjusted her bikini top while Blaine grinned smugly with noted arrogance.

"Problem, Murdock?" Blaine casually asked.

"Yeah, sexcapades in front of the other guests," Murdock announced. "If you can't behave in the public areas, take it up to your room."

"Is someone complaining?" Blaine demanded.

"Yeah, I'm complaining," Murdock remarked with increasing agitation. "This isn't wild kingdom. Show some respect for our other guests."

"Someone needs to get laid," Patrice muttered.

He shot a glare at the voluptuous woman in the hot tub alongside Blaine. "You think I'm joking?" Murdock snarled hotly while pointing a warning finger at her then pointed away from the hotel. "You can take your little frat party to the motel on the highway, if you have a problem with it."

Blaine managed a nervous laugh and attempted to smooth things over. "No, we're good," he announced. "We'll take it up to our room."

Blaine and Patrice climbed out of the hot tub, grabbed their towels, and hastily dried off while walking across the terrace. Murdock shook his head with disgust then looked at Dane and smiled timidly.

"Sorry, that won't happen again," Murdock gently informed him.

Dane stared at Murdock, having witnessed the mild mannered man driven to a hostile eruption. Dane smiled timidly and gave a slight nod. Alicia glanced at Murdock as he walked away then looked back at Dane and grinned.

"So," she cooed and pressed against him, "where were we?"

Harley walked onto the terrace, approached Murdock as he was about to leave, and hastily pulled him aside. Dane appeared interested in their conversation despite Alicia's attempt to cozy up to him. Across the terrace, not far from the poolside lobby entrance, Blaine continued to dry himself with an official hotel towel while remaining equally interested in the interaction between Murdock and Harley. Patrice finished drying herself then noted Blaine's intent stare at the owner and her friend. She eyed Blaine and appeared curious.

"Got eyes for the little princess?"

Blaine suddenly snapped out of his trance and looked at Patrice with surprise. "What? No, of course not."

"Then what has you so interested?" she asked while raising a clever brow. "Certainly you don't secretly desire Murdock."

Blaine rolled his eyes and shoved Patrice toward the lobby entrance. "Your mind never leaves the gutter, does it?"

She casually shrugged then grinned. "I'm pretty sure my mind being in the gutter is the only reason you guys invited me to this remote resort hell."

He firmly indicated the door, clearly annoyed. She flaunted a smile and headed for the door. On the other side of the terrace, Harley stopped Murdock near one of the marble benches not far from the pool. He noted the defeated look on her face.

"I've been trying to contact support for my tablet, but the phones don't appear to be working now either," Harley informed him with concern. "Add one more thing to our growing list of problems." She ran her fingers through her hair and groaned softly. "Can I use your cell phone to contact the phone company?"

Murdock fished his cell phone from his pocket and handed it to her. "You realize you'll have to go to the roof or drive halfway to town to get a signal on that."

"Yeah, I know, but I don't know what else to do," Harley replied with a dreary sigh. "I swear Remy did something to the computer. Now I can't get into the system at all."

"You know what the problem is, don't you?"

"Yeah, she's mean and manipulative."

"No, it's that lighthouse," he informed her while pointing to the mammoth tower not far from the terrace. "It interferes with anything wireless. You should turn off the beacon."

Harley's look hardened to his suggestion. "You know I can't do that."

"I know why you think you have to--"

She felt her hostility rising. "I said no, Murdock."

"It's been a year, Harley," he announced softly with sadness in his eyes. "They're *not* lost at sea. That beacon won't help them find their way home. You have to accept that and stop torturing yourself."

"Yeah, well, it's my beacon," she scoffed then spun on her heels and stormed away from him.

Murdock groaned, ran his fingers through his hair, and then hurried after her. Alicia looked across the terrace as Harley and Murdock headed for the glass doors and entered the lobby. She looked back at Dane, grinned, and affectionately kissed his neck.

"You seem awfully distracted," she remarked while attempting to arouse him by caressing his bare chest. "What has you so preoccupied?"

Dane looked back at the glass lobby doors and barely noticed Alicia's caressing hands. "Nothing, it's just--" He suddenly tensed and looked back at the love-starved woman pawing at him. "I have a lot on my mind right now, that's all." Dane stopped her traveling hands, surprising her. "I'm afraid I'm not very good company tonight." He attempted a weak smile. "Could I bow out gracefully just for tonight? There's, uh, something I need to do before it gets too late."

Alicia was stunned by the request and mechanically straightened. "Really?" She immediately fidgeted then forced a weak smile. "I mean, of course. I have an early morning appraisal anyway," she replied. "I'll change then head home, okay?"

Dane stared into her eyes and tensed, possibly kicking himself for brushing her off. "I'm really sorry, Alicia."

"No, I understand," she quickly interjected and managed a smile. "Your store is going to open next week and you have your own house in the city to close on. You're under a lot of pressure." She gently tilted her head and gave him a slightly concerned look. "We're still on for dinner tomorrow, right?"

"Yes, of course," he replied more naturally and even smiled. "I'll pick you up at your place around six."

"I'll see you then."

Alicia kissed him warmly but passionately on the lips. Dane returned the kiss but remained distracted. He watched her slip out of the hot tub, catching an eyeful of her thong bikini bottom, and withheld his soft whimper. As she grabbed a towel and walked away, he uncertainly ran his fingers through his hair.

"What the hell is wrong with you, Dane?" he muttered softly to himself.

Dane glanced back toward the glass lobby windows, stared into the lobby, and watched as Alicia disappeared near the elevators. His eyes then strayed to Harley as she approached the desk. He studied her a long, silent moment, groaned softly, and sank down in the tub. A chilling breeze blew past him. Dane opened his eyes and quickly looked around. On the terrace not far from the kitchen entrance, he saw someone disappear between the overgrown hedges in desperate need of trimming. Dane became curious and hurried from the hot tub. He grabbed a towel and dried himself as he headed across the terrace in the direction of the hedges. He suddenly hesitated and looked down. Bloody work boot prints headed in the same direction, causing Dane to stop and reconsider his current path. As he stared at the bloody boot prints, they appeared to vanish before his eyes and then reappear further ahead, leading along the path between the overgrown hedges. Dane reconsidered following but kept his eyes on the boot prints. They completely vanished before his eyes.

"And on that note, I'm going to lock myself in my room," he muttered softly while staring at the clean, stone terrace.

Dane tossed his towel onto a nearby lounge chair and hastily slipped into his shirt and shoes. He then heard a faint thud in the distance beyond the hedges. He hesitated a moment, groaned at his own curiosity, and then headed across the terrace toward the path between the hedges. He cautiously slipped between the hedges, which nearly blocked the entire path, and appeared within a small, overgrown garden not far from the caretaker's workshop. He glanced around the quiet, empty area then looked toward the tasteful, split rail fencing along the cliff. Dane approached the fencing, placed his hand on the top railing, and peered over the edge.

It was a two hundred yard drop down to the rocky infested water below. At the very bottom, there appeared to be a body lying broken on the rocks. Dane gasped with surprise and leaned over the fence for a closer look. Whatever he had seen was no longer there. Dane took a step away from the fence then hesitated and looked at the professionally made sign tacked to the post. It read, 'Please do not climb the fence. Support is just a phone call away.' It was followed by the phone number to a suicide hotline. Dane looked from the sign to the fence and the sharp drop-off just beyond it. It was chilling to think such a sign was necessary.

Chapter Six

*D*ane entered his guestroom from the attached bathroom. He was now freshly showered and changed into a pair of comfortable, lounge around shorts. He finished drying his hair with the plush, white towel and carelessly tossed it onto the nearby chair. He hesitated, eyed the damp towel, and then groaned. He picked up the towel and returned it to the bathroom.

"I'll make someone a fine wife one day," he muttered then approached the bed.

Dane pulled the covers down to reveal the entire right side of the bed saturated with a huge bloodstain. The bloodstain, indicating a massacre had occurred in that very bed, wasn't visible to him. He casually slipped beneath the fresh, crisp covers, made himself comfortable, and picked up the old, leather-bound book that had once been located in the lobby. Admittedly, he was a historical nerd. He skimmed through the first few pages then found something of interest regarding the hotel.

Within the pages of the book, he was taken back over one hundred years to a time just before the hotel was built. The lighthouse was located in its rightful place near the edge of the cliff.

Its powerful beacon shined through the raging storm. It was a fierce storm like no other. The small dwelling attached to the lighthouse had seen better days and appeared abandoned. Within the lighthouse lantern room, three scruffy, bearded men in their mid-forties sat on old crates and passed a bottle of whiskey around. All three were clearly drunk and sought shelter within the lighthouse during the horrific storm. It was only sheer luck that one of them happened upon a bottle of whiskey stashed in an old desk within the dilapidated caretaker's house. The three men were long-time friends, shipmates on an old fishing trawler that was now anchored just off shore. The dinghy used to transfer them from the ship in the harsh storm was pulled several yards on shore and turned upside down in an effort to keep it from being dragged out to sea.

The three similarly dressed sailors, Albert, Edward, and Walter, barely noticed the storm in their drunken condition. They laughed and had a good time. It wasn't the first time the three men had spent a drunken evening together while waiting out a fierce storm. The wind blew harshly against the glass surrounding them, finally reminding them of the wild storm just outside.

"Think she's still there?" Albert asked while grinning at his comment.

"Our lady can brave the toughest storms," Edward announced then laughed. "Tough old broad."

Walter groaned softly and attempted to stand in his drunken condition. He struggled to maintain his balance, stumbled slightly, and then laughed at himself.

"I'll have a look," Walter announced.

He strained to look out the dirty window pelted with rain as the wind forced the water against the glass, resembling a small waterfall. It made seeing outside difficult. He appeared momentarily stunned at what he thought he saw and looked again.

"Lord," he cried out. "I think she's been torn in half. Her running lights are scattered everywhere."

The two other men struggled to stand, nearly knocking each other over in the process. They stumbled to the window and strained to look out as well.

"That's not our girl," Albert cried out and smacked Walter on the arm then pointed with such vigor it nearly knocked him down. "There's another ship out there, you idiot!"

"Awfully close to the rocks," Edward remarked.

All three men strained to see the location of the ship braving the heavy waves in a field of scattered rocks. Their shared expression was that of concern.

"They can't see a damned thing," Walter suddenly announced with horror then indicated the light above them. "The beacon isn't cutting through the storm. Those rocks are practically in front of their faces, and they can't see them!"

"We have the lanterns," Edward announced. "We could go out there--"

"Oh, hell!"

The cargo ship crashed into the rocks, swiping its side, and tearing into the hull as it passed. The rough waves launched the ship back into the rocks for a second strike. All three men stood in the lantern room, horror on their faces, as they helplessly watched the cargo ship rapidly sink. Despite what seemed a lifetime, the three men sprang into action only a minute later. They lit their lanterns and stumbled for the lighthouse stairs.

Once outside, all three men stumbled through the wet sand after braving the treacherous wooden stairs built into the side of the cliff from the lighthouse above. They reached the rough surf and waved their lanterns. None could see the remains of the ship, but it was possible some survivors would see their lanterns and make it to shore. Despite being soaked in the pouring rain for nearly an hour, no survivors made it to shore. The crew of the cargo ship had been lost at sea.

The following morning was bright and sunny, giving no indication that a violent storm had taken down an entire ship, claiming the lives of so many. The three men pulled the dinghy toward the surf. Surprisingly, their ship remained intact and anchored offshore. Debris from the sunken cargo ship had already made its way to shore, although no bodies had been recovered. A nearly destroyed launch barely made it to shore, but it was obvious there was something within the broken boat. Curious, all three men headed for the shattered launch partway in the surf. They stared with bewilderment at the sight.

A small chest weighted down the remaining boat. The mere fact that it was there indicated someone went to great lengths to remove the chest from the sinking ship. The same thought occurred to all three men. They ran into the surf and pulled the nearly destroyed launch to shore. Within minutes, they cracked open the thick lock on the chest and pulled back the lid. All three men stared with shared disbelief and the small chest filled with gold coins. They exchanged looks then began laughing while hugging one another.

Two years later, the hotel had been built and the three men were now owners of the property above and below the cliffs. Neither had mentioned witnessing the ship sinking nor the treasure they had found that stormy night. It was rumored that they had hid the remaining treasure within the recently constructed hotel for safekeeping until they could slowly introduce their newly found wealth as income from the hotel. Although best friends and shipmates, greed and differences of opinion on how to spend the money became an issue.

One year later. Early in the evening, the teenage caretaker trimmed the hedges alongside the hotel. Ernest was a lanky kid with short hair and a days' worth of stubble on his face. His work overalls were stained with grass and dirt, indicating the amount of labor he put into his job. The summer season hadn't officially started, so the hotel was pleasantly quiet. Apart from the sounds of crashing waves from the ocean below, the snipping of the caretaker's manual hedge clippers was the only sound from the hotel.

The sounds of raised voices broke the silence, catching the young man's attention. He straightened and strained to listen to the familiar male voices from within the lobby. He stepped onto the terrace, realizing by the sounds of it, that the argument had turned violent. Someone yelled out. It was a painful howl, alerting the groundskeeper to something horrible beyond the wall of glass. He ran to the terrace doors as several gunshots rang out. A bullet pierced the window not inches from the young man's head. He hesitated and reconsidered entering. Everything suddenly became deathly quiet. The young man slowly opened the terrace door and stepped into the lobby. The three hotel owners lie on the stone floor, blood seeping from their bodies and collecting into large pools. All three were dead.

Chapter Seven

*T*wenty years after the mass slaying of the three friends, the hotel had been owned and operated by the only surviving relatives of Albert, which were Harley's great grandparents. With the hotel's booming business during the spring and summer season, Harley's great grandparents took a well-deserved vacation and left the hotel in the capable hands of their faithful caretaker and groundskeeper, Ernest. He was assisted by a small off-season crew. The skeleton crew consisted of the Ernest and his wife, Agnes, who maintained the bills and paperwork. There was also the cook and one of the younger, live-in maids. The young maid, Irene, entered the kitchen and uncertainly approached Mildred. The pleasantly plump, middle-aged cook noted the strange look on the young maid's face.

"Is everything okay, dear?" Mildred asked the attractive young maid.

"Ernest has been making a lot of insane accusations the last few days," Irene replied with a concerned look on her youthful face. "He keeps rambling on about ghosts."

"That's nothing new," Mildred replied and waved off the young maid. "He's been talking that crazy nonsense for the last twenty years."

"Well, as long as you're sure he's okay," Irene announced timidly, although she didn't appear convinced. "I hadn't seen Agnes all morning. She said she'd help me with some of the guestroom curtains."

"The poor girl was up half the night with a migraine," Mildred informed her. "She probably overslept. Will you be a dear and wake her for me?"

"Sure," Irene replied then left the kitchen in the direction of the staff wing.

The staff wing corridor was normally quiet during off-season, since only four employees remained to keep the hotel running. The caretaker and his wife had a suite halfway down the hallway. As senior staff, they were given the larger suite with a nicer view. The young maid paused before the door and promptly knocked on it. Irene immediately regretted the firm knock, sensitive to the idea of Agnes suffering from a migraine. When there was no response, she knocked a little louder, causing the door to jolt open. Irene was surprised by the door not being shut tight or even locked as she thought it should be. The young maid slowly pushed open the door and announced herself while doing so.

"Agnes?" she called out and listened for the sound of a running shower, but she didn't hear anything. It was unusually quiet. "It's Irene. Are you awake?"

There was no response. Irene debated leaving or investigating. If Agnes' condition were more serious than a migraine, it would be wise to check on her, just to be safe. The young maid approached the partially open bedroom door and tapped softly on it while slowly pushing it open.

"Are you awake?"

As Irene peered into the bedroom, she saw Agnes partially beneath the blood-soaked sheets. The bed, headboard, and wall were strewn with blood spatters. The tears in the sheets indicated she'd been attacked while she slept. Agnes lie sprawled across the bed in a slightly unnatural position with her eyes and her mouth opened as if in mid-scream. Several deep cuts to her lower arms and hands indicated she had made an attempt to fight off her attacker. The young maid stifled her scream, immediately turning and running from the room. She thundered down the long hallway and headed for the kitchen screaming for Mildred the entire way. She was certain the woman had to have heard her screams. Irene entered the kitchen and came to an abrupt stop, nearly falling to the floor having slipped in fresh blood. Irene followed the streak of blood with her eyes and saw the cook lying partially behind the island counter, her hand still clutching a dishtowel now soaked in her own blood. Irene screamed and swiftly spun around, colliding with the caretaker.

She was about to speak when she saw he was covered in blood while holding a bloodied ax. Irene screamed at the blank look on the caretaker's face, spattered with blood. Without emotion, he swung the ax, impaling her in the chest, and immediately pulled it free. Irene clutched her bleeding chest as the blood poured between her fingers, running down her neatly pressed uniform. As she slowly sank, he followed her to the floor, repeatedly striking her with the blood-soaked ax. Once she lie motionless on the floor, he continued his brutal assault, flinging blood across the kitchen with each recoil. While on his knees over the mutilated young woman, he stared at her blood-covered body without remorse or expression. The caretaker slowly straightened, stepped over the dead girl's body, and headed for the back door. He dragged the bloodied ax alongside him, leaving bloody boot prints and a streak of blood as the ax grinded along the tile.

The caretaker crossed the terrace, at which time was without a pool or hot tub, and headed toward the caretaker's workshop, leaving behind a trail of bloody footprints. He dropped the bloodstained ax on the stone as he approached his workshop. Ernest stopped before the wood chipper and turned it on. It made a loud whirring sound.

✝

*P*resent day. Dane stared at the open book he held on his lap while appearing tense where he remained within his bed. He shut the book and looked slightly stunned by what he had just read regarding the hotel's history.

"I can see why they don't put that on the hotel's website," he muttered.

He set the book on the nightstand, turned off the light by the base, and collapsed onto his back. He stared at the ceiling a moment then turned toward the right side of the bed. He faced a young, naked dead woman covered in blood. Her eyes were open as she stared at him with horror permanently frozen on her face. He was unable to see the dead woman lying in the bed alongside him. Dane nuzzled his pillow and attempted to sleep. A cold chill sent a shiver down his spine. He quickly sat up in bed, turned on the light, and looked toward the windows. None were open. He looked around the room and then to the clean, white sheets on the bed alongside him. He stared at the spot the dead woman once occupied and uncertainly ran his hand over the bed. He again shivered. He pulled the covers back and stared at the empty, clean bed alongside him but didn't appear convinced.

Chapter Eight

Midnight. Harley stood behind the large check-in desk and attempted to work on the computer with frustration clearly on her face. She'd once again lost track of time while fighting with the new system Remy installed. For something that was supposed to be an improvement, it was merely a source of stress for Harley. She wanted to throw the computer off the cliff, but she convinced herself that would be counterproductive.

"Stupid piece of shit--"

She glanced up and saw Dane standing just outside the elevators watching her. That was embarrassing. She smiled timidly and tensed at his mysterious appearance. She hadn't heard the elevator's usual ding announcing its arrival, nor did she hear the doors opening, which she always heard when it was late at night and excessively quiet in the lobby.

"Sorry," she announced gently, embarrassed having been caught using foul language around the guests. "Electronics and I aren't getting along these days."

"Trust me, I know the feeling."

Dane reluctantly approached her and the desk while keeping his gaze fixed upon her. Harley studied his expression, humored by his unusual mannerism.

"You look at me as if I'm going to bite you," she teased. Something then occurred to Harley and it troubled her. "Has Remy been spreading gossip about me? She's been a little testy about working so many evenings lately."

"No, she hasn't mentioned you at all," he announced and started to relax.

"Oh, that's good. She's one of my dearest friends; I'd hate to have to fire her," Harley teased then returned to the computer. She pounded on the keyboard with frustration then pushed it away, finally giving up.

"Computers can be vengeful," he remarked casually and offered a timid smile. "Would you like me to have a look at it? I'm quite good with electronics."

"Be my guest," she muttered with defeat.

Dane rounded the desk and joined her on the other side. Whereas most men seemed to invade her personal space, Dane was reluctant to move too close. Harley took a step back, allowing him some space to work. She resisted moving too many steps away from him, since she didn't want to give the impression that she had a problem with him. Dane typed onto the keyboard and easily pulled up the hotel's property management system. Harley watched then found herself eyeing him with equal interest. She often avoided standing too close to strangers, feeling they gave off a strange vibe. She didn't get that cringe worthy vibe from Dane, but she wasn't sure why.

Something about him was comforting, almost the way she felt around Murdock. Although, she was very much aware he wasn't Murdock. She stood almost close enough to feel the heat from his body, and it was extremely pleasant. Faint traces of expensive cologne lingered on his clothes. The scent was rather stimulating. She felt compelled to glance at his profile as he worked on the computer. Far from hunky actor handsome, he was appealing in a hard to explain way. It seemed odd. She hadn't remembered the last time she looked at a man and marveled at his attractiveness. There was a good chance if he touched her, she wouldn't pull away as her usual reaction toward men. Dane glanced at her over his shoulder and seemed almost surprised by her closeness. She smiled in response. It would seem he had nearly as many hang-ups as she had.

Dane looked back at the screen and smiled, although reluctant to let her notice.

"What were you attempting to do?" he finally asked.

"I wanted to check our summer reservations," Harley replied and now watched the screen instead of the man standing before it. "Remy updated the entire system, so I'm not even sure--"

Dane tapped onto the keyboard. The reservations for the summer appeared on the screen. Harley was stunned at how easily he was able to manipulate the computer with which she'd spent so many hours fighting.

"I'll be damned," she announced with surprise then grinned. "You're like a genius or something."

"I'll go with 'or something'."

She wanted to sneak another peek at the man alongside her, but something on the screen caught her eye. Her expression faded to concern. "No, this can't be. There aren't any reservations for the summer," she gasped and nearly went into panic mode. "I swore we were already half-booked the last time I looked. This can't be accurate. Without our summer reservations, I won't be able to keep the hotel going another season." Her mind was racing as she stared at the numbers on the screen. "The bank won't approve my improvement loan. I'll lose the hotel!"

Dane stared at her with a strange look then glanced back at the computer and tapped a few keys.

"I think you're worrying over nothing," he gently informed her in a calm, reassuring tone. "This hasn't been updated. I guess Remy hadn't gotten that far. I'm sure you're right about the hotel being half-booked." He pressed a button, allowing the property management screen to disappear then turned to face her. "You should probably just ask Remy about it in the morning."

She finally tore her eyes away from the computer screen and barely glanced at Dane. Harley was feeling depressed after what she'd seen.

"If she'll talk to me," she muttered and wearily leaned on the desk. "I'm so tired."

He studied her a moment and appeared curious. "It's late. Why don't you go to bed?"

"I would, but I can't sleep," she muttered and rested her chin on her fist. "Too much stress, I suppose. I come for a long line of insomniacs."

"I assume you're under a great burden trying to run this big hotel by yourself."

She groaned softly and straightened. "Murdock does his best to help."

"The man I met at the hot tub?" Dane asked while tilting his head. "Is he your boyfriend?"

Harley met his gaze and held back her laugh. "No, we're just friends." She felt relaxed for the first time. "I love Murdock more than life itself, but I'm not ready to become romantically involved with him." Harley inhaled deeply and sighed. "It's kind of ironic, because I don't believe in true love, but I'm still holding out hope it exists."

Dane stared at Harley with a strange expression on his face. She smiled with embarrassment and looked away.

"I know that look," she announced while holding back her laugh. "You think I'm young and naive."

"I suppose I do, but I also believe true love exists," he firmly informed her. "I'm guessing you don't get out much, so your list of potential boyfriends is probably limited."

"I can't remember the last time I went anywhere. I've been too busy trying to keep this white elephant afloat." She rested heavily against the desk and stared at him while grinning. "What's it like to be successful? I'd really love to know."

"My success was a fluke," he casually informed her. "I was a struggling archaeologist living in boarding houses between digs. On my last dig, everyone bailed out after our funding was drained. Being the stubborn, thick-headed idiot I am, I stuck it out on my own dime." He grinned and held back his chuckle. "Nearly out of water and on my third straight day without anything to eat that didn't crawl, I saw this brilliant light. I assumed I was having a stroke. Turns out it was the biggest and rarest diamond you could ever imagine. Every billionaire on every continent wanted a piece of my diamond."

"Oh, my God," she gasped. "What did you do?"

"I became a world famous jeweler overnight," he informed her. "I designed my own settings, cut that baby apart, and sold my creations to the highest bidders."

"And you want to live in our hick town?" she suddenly questioned. "I think you're putting me on."

"Would you believe world famous this side of the Mississippi?"

She laughed softly. "I'd be willing to believe that," she replied. "Explains why Alicia's glowing too." Harley suddenly straightened and held back her alarm. "Oh, I shouldn't have said that. I'm sorry. I didn't mean to imply--"

"Imply what? That Alicia is only interested in my diamonds?" he teased. "It's okay. I figured that out the first time she smiled at me. I'd be lying if I said I didn't enjoy the attention. I never had much time for relationships and high-maintenance women. It's nice to know I can finally afford both." He appeared humored at the thought. "Poor girl. She's going to be terribly disappointed when she learns everything I have is tied up in my store's inventory and the house I'm buying."

Harley had to laugh at the comment. "I was almost rich once," she announced then grinned slyly. "A guy offered me a few million dollars for the hotel. Murdock thought I was crazy to turn it down. I suppose I enjoy my low-maintenance lifestyle." She shrugged without care and held back her laugh. "At least I know who my friends are. They're the ones buying my groceries and unclogging my toilets."

They both laughed. Dane sighed while appearing weary from the late hour.

"I suppose that's the difference between men and women," he remarked. "My friends wanted to see how fast they could spend my money. My so-called best friend, Collin, threw me into the fast lane." He gave her a curious look. "Have you ever looked back at your life and pinpointed the exact moment your world turned to crap?"

Harley snorted a laugh. "Does every other day count?"

"My particular undoing was a ritzy party about a year ago," he remarked and drifted out a moment while shaking his head. "A fast but thankfully brief downward spiral into the bowels of hell courtesy of my best friend, Collin."

"What could be so bad?" Harley nearly gasped.

"Expensive trashy women and a month-long drunken stupor," he casually replied. "One month living like a rock star nearly killed me. I quit cold turkey and hope I never return to that lifestyle again."

Harley studied him a moment then managed a tiny smile. "Is that why you sent Alicia home?"

Dane looked at her with surprise and immediately fidgeted. Harley felt the color rise to her cheeks, feeling his tension.

"I'm sorry," she quickly announced. "That was an inappropriate thing to ask."

"No," he replied gently and straightened proudly. "You pretty much hit that nail on the head."

"So when you say you quit cold turkey--?" she asked and raised her brow in silent question.

"Pretty much everything," he replied. "Booze, women, and Collin." Dane studied her a moment, snorted a soft laugh, and shook his head. "I can't believe I actually admitted that aloud--to a woman no less."

"Guys seem inclined to tell me all their dirty little secrets. I never understood why," she announced while grinning. "Murdock's been out of that game longer than you have. You've got nothing to be embarrassed about."

Dane appeared embarrassed and quickly attempted to change the subject. "I, uh, was reading that book on the town's history," he informed her while fidgeting slightly. "I was a little shocked at some of the hotel's more violent history."

"Oh, you mean the murders," Harley announced then offered a tiny smile. "This place had a bad rap for a few decades, to say the least. Thankfully, our last scandalous murder/suicide was nearly thirty years ago."

"The young couple who sought shelter here during a storm in off-season?"

"Yeah," Harley replied with a dreary sigh.

"You wouldn't happen to know which room they were staying in by chance?" he asked while fidgeting slightly.

"I was never given that information," she replied while offering a tiny smile. "My mother was only about sixteen years old when that happened. My grandparents were still in change back then." Harley shook her head. "Ironically, my mother remembered them as being a nice, young couple recently married."

"The book was fuzzy on the details," Dane announced.

"Not many details to mention," she replied. "The night they checked in, the husband was hanging out with my grandfather playing pool while his bride was 'resting'. When he returned to their room, he caught his bride in bed with our young gardener. Her husband shot them both several times then turned the gun on himself."

"So, uh, who's the gardener now?" Dane asked while tilting his head. "Sounds like trouble seems to follow the person holding that position. I think I'd like to avoid him."

"Murdock tends to mostly everything during off-season," she replied. "You're safe though. He's not a psycho killer."

"What about those other suicides?"

Harley groaned softly and shook her head. "We get our occasional jumper. People travel miles to jump off the cliff." She sighed softly.

"I noticed the suicide hotline number posted on the fence along the cliff," Dane remarked and fidgeted slightly. "Honestly, I thought it was a joke."

"No," Harley replied with a sigh. "Sadly, the beauty and symbolism attracts jumpers. It somehow appeals to them. Thankfully, the suicidal rate off that cliff has declined since we posted that sign. I'd like to think it forces them to re-evaluate taking that leap."

"Perhaps."

Rhodes mysteriously appeared before the desk, startling Harley and Dane. Just his presence alone was enough to startle Harley, but in the middle of the night, he was twice as creepy.

"I've been trying to call down here all night," Rhodes informed her with an annoyed tone. "What's with the phones?"

"I'm not sure," she announced and attempted to keep from being intimidated by the brawny man. "We'll have someone out to look at the system in the morning. Is there something I can do for you, Rhodes?"

Rhodes glared at Dane, who stared back with a strange look. He returned his attention to Harley. "The shower in my room isn't working."

"I'm sorry to hear that. I'll have Murdock look at it in the morning," Harley replied.

"It's not working *tonight*," Rhodes snarled.

"I can certainly change rooms for you, but there's nothing I can do about a broken shower until morning."

"Why don't you come up and at least look at it?" he demanded as his eyes pierced through her.

His look caused her to shiver. Despite being handsome, he was frightening. "There's nothing I can do more than you can," Harley insisted. "Murdock will look at it in the morning. Did you want another room?"

"No."

Rhodes glared at Dane, who was compelled to stare back. He then turned and headed back toward the elevators.

Harley watched him and insecurely rubbed her arms. "That guy gives me the chills."

"He didn't do much for me either," Dane muttered. "Who is that?"

"That's Rhodes," she moaned softly. "He's part of the frat party you were subjected to tonight in the hot tub."

"Oh, uh, the couple engaging in sexcapades."

She looked at him with surprise by the comment. "My God, you sound like Murdock," she remarked then laughed softly. "Yes, that couple. Blaine and Patrice. There's one more nightmare to their group, Decker. They've been drunk and disorderly every night since they've been here."

Dane appeared curious. "How long have they been here?"

"Seems like forever," she muttered then frowned. "Don't be surprised if you see Patrice making out with a different guy each night. I think she's their communal girlfriend."

"Hmm, gross."

"Tell me about it," she groaned softly. "I've walked in on their drunken adventures on more than one occasion. Been asked to join in more than once too." Harley frowned with disgust. "They're not too bad during the day, but once night falls, it's pretty disturbing. Rhodes is just dying to get me alone. I know it. Murdock is going to throw them out soon."

"I don't blame him." Dane straightened proudly. "If you run into any trouble, I'm here."

"I appreciate that, Dane."

"I realize I don't look like much, but I was bullied a lot as a kid," he informed her. "I've learned to handle myself over the years."

"I believe you can. Thank you."

She kissed him on the cheek, startling him. He looked ready to bolt from the room. Harley grinned and appeared humored at his surprise.

"That's cute," she teased. "You still think I'm going to bite you." Harley sighed softly and ran her fingers lazily through her hair. "I think I'm actually tired enough to fall asleep." She offered a warm smile. "Goodnight, Dane."

Dane watched Harley head for the corridor near the elevators then smiled to himself. As she disappeared around the corner, he suddenly frowned and shook his head.

"What the hell are you doing, Dane?" he muttered softly.

Chapter Nine

$\mathcal{E}$arly the following morning, the simple continental breakfast was served on top of the bar within the formal lounge. Despite the massive bar, the lounge hadn't served alcohol in nearly two years. Its current function was a breakfast bar for hotel guests. Although the lounge could comfortably seat one hundred guests, little space was needed for the few off-season guests staying within the hotel. The formal banquet hall was located on the opposite end of the corridor and could hold at least two hundred guests. Although it had been used for many gatherings and parties in the hotel's past, the banquet hall had been locked and remained unused since Harley's parents died as well.

Remy arranged fresh fruit in a bowl on the bar and kept busy with her morning routine. A married couple in their late thirties, Kaplan and Bernie Gooding, sat at one of the small, round tables and sipped their coffee. Bernie was the definition of high maintenance. Her strawberry blond hair came straight from a beauty parlor, as did her false nails. She wore enough make-up to give the illusion of beauty, but without make-up, she'd almost certainly look older than her years. She was a voluptuous woman, wearing expensive clothes that accentuated her curves. Her husband, Kaplan, was a distinguished looking man with thinning light brown hair, which he attempted to comb strategically over the thinning spots. He was an average build and height, although it was obvious he'd given up exercise after marriage. The couple glanced casually around the room, giving an almost bored appearance. Bernie then leaned closer to her husband to speak freely.

"This place is a gold mine," she announced in a hushed tone, barely able to contain her enthusiasm. "The woodwork in every room must have been carved by hand."

"That girl has no idea what this hotel is worth," Kaplan informed his wife while attempting to keep his voice down as well. "Sure, it needs some work, but the structure itself is amazing. The possibilities are endless."

"What do you think?" Bernie asked softly while darting looks around the room to ensure no one was within earshot. "Should we make an offer on the place?"

"We'll need to get a hold of that real estate agent," Kaplan replied equally soft. "There's no way that girl can hold onto this place for very long. She can't even break even without the necessary upkeep and improvements. She's never going to get that business improvement loan."

"Didn't you say she had an offer on the hotel before and turned it down?" Bernie whispered.

"Yeah, but that was shortly after her parents died," he replied. "A lot has changed since then. She can't keep this place going."

Bernie again looked around, attempting to hide her enthusiasm. "This place is fantastic, Kaplan. It's perfect," she announced softly almost under her breath. "We must get our hands on it."

"We will," he replied while acting disinterested. "We just need to play it smart."

Harley and Murdock entered the room while playfully bantering and pushing each other. Murdock grabbed Harley around the waist and attempted to toss her over his shoulder. She screamed playfully, alerting the quietly seated couple. Kaplan and Bernie glared their disapproval. Harley firmly tapped Murdock on the shoulder. He put her down and acted innocent. Remy ignored them and left the room.

"Did you feel that cold wind blow past?" Murdock teased while staring after Remy.

"Yes, I did."

Kaplan motioned them to their table with his usual insistence. Harley hid her grimace and approached with a smile while Murdock checked out the coffee situation.

"How's breakfast?" Harley cheerfully asked.

"The coffee is bitter and the eggs are runny," Bernie replied in a slightly snobbish tone.

"I'll mention it to Remy," Harley remarked while attempting not to grit her teeth.

"About those party animals you call guests--" Kaplan began but was interrupted.

"I'm sorry about them, Kaplan," Harley announced. "If you prefer, I'm willing to move you clear across the hotel."

"Why should I have to switch rooms?" Kaplan demanded. "I finally found one with the perfect view and proper firmness in the mattress. Move them."

"Yeah, right out the door," Murdock muttered as he approached without his usual coffee.

"Murdock," Harley scolded softly.

"It's about time," Bernie scoffed in a high-pitched squeal. "Night after night until all hours."

"I thought the hotel offered free Wi-Fi?" Kaplan demanded, his irritation rising. "I can't even logon."

"We've been having trouble with the phones as well as the internet," Harley politely informed him. "I promise we'll have someone out to look at it today."

"I swear you said that yesterday."

"It's off-season," Harley gently informed him. "Things aren't running as smoothly as they do during the tourist season. On the bright side, it's going to be warm and sunny today. The beach should be nice."

"Unfortunately the water will be freezing," Kaplan countered while sneering.

"I'd better find Remy and let her know about the coffee," Harley announced and left their table in a hurry.

Murdock offered a timid smile at the irritating couple then hurried after Harley. Murdock caught up with Harley as she left the lounge and entered the corridor.

"They're not happy unless they're complaining about something," Murdock muttered.

"I can't wait for them to check out," Harley replied. "We need guests; just not those guests. I swear they're only staying to push my buttons."

"I'm going to see if Remy needs any help in the kitchen," Murdock announced then gave her a curious look. "Do you have the front desk today?"

"Yeah, I've got the desk," Harley replied with a dreary sigh. "I need to catch up on my reading anyway."

Chapter Ten

*L*ater that afternoon, Harley entered the kitchen and looked around for Murdock or Remy. Both were suspiciously absent for what seemed a long time. The kitchen was one of the first places to look for either when they were missing. Remy would occasionally take her book onto the terrace to read, but she mostly stayed within the lobby to keep herself readily available to the guests. When they had no guests, all three tended to hang out on the terrace or head down to the beach when it was warm and sunny.

"Remy? Murdock?" she called while looking around the massive kitchen.

She crossed the kitchen and hesitated just near the island counter. As she stared at the tile floor, blood seeped through the grout and swiftly collected into a large pool. Harley held her breath, shut her eyes a moment, and then opened them. The blood was gone. She exhaled softly and continued across the kitchen. She heard a strange scraping sound, which immediately alerted her. Harley spun around to face the main entrance. She wasn't surprised when she didn't find anything or anyone there.

The kitchen was particularly creepy when she found herself alone there. She seldom heard or saw things when she was in the company of her friends or the seasonal staff. She always found it interesting that no one else ever complained about paranormal activity. How was it possible that she was the only one to witness such things? The back door creaked open, startling her. She glanced at the kitchen door leading to the terrace not far from the pool and the caretaker's workshop. She heard the strange scraping sound again, but there was nothing there. Harley shivered slightly and rubbed her chilled shoulders. She hurried to the door to shut it.

As she stared out to the terrace and the nearby hot tub, she saw bloodied boot prints and a strange line of blood alongside the footprints. She could hear the faint sound of a machine running somewhere near the caretaker's workshop. Harley drew a deep breath and stepped onto the terrace. She uncertainly followed the bloodied boot prints past the hot tub and toward the path between the overgrown hedges. As she passed through the hedges, she paused and stared at the caretaker's workshop off to the right, opposite the fenced off cliff. The old wood chipper roared loudly as rusted gears grinded with a hideous sound. Harley uncertainly approached the old wood chipper and watched it vibrate. Bloodstains covered the entire output chute.

The chipper suddenly fell silent. It hadn't run in years, so she was certain it was only her imagination or perhaps the ghosts screwing with her again. She rubbed her shoulders while staring at the monstrosity. The caretaker's workshop had always given her the chills. She didn't want to remain there any longer than necessary and certainly not by herself. Harley quickly turned and collided with Murdock. Harley let out a startled scream, alarming Murdock as well. He clutched his chest and gasped softly as Harley attempted to relax.

"Damn it, I wish you'd stop doing that," Murdock gasped as he finally released his chest. "You're going to give me a heart attack one of these days."

"Maybe you should stop sneaking up on me then," she launched back, unable to shake the chills this time. "What are you doing out here anyway?"

"I saw you heading this way," he informed her. "I called, but I guess you didn't hear me."

She gave him a bewildered look. Was it possible she didn't hear him calling her? She found that a little hard to believe, but

Murdock wouldn't make up stories, and he certainly wouldn't scare her on purpose. It wasn't his style. He stared at her and appeared curious.

"Come on," he announced in a sympathetic tone then tilted his head while giving her his best puppy dog eyes. "What's going on with you lately? Whatever it is, you can tell me."

She frowned and avoided looking at him. "You'd never believe me."

Murdock drew a deep breath. "Ghosts again?"

Harley glared at him with disappointment. "I knew you wouldn't believe me."

He placed his arm around her, pulled her to his side, and kissed her forehead. "Yeah, you're a few cards short of a full deck, but if you think you're seeing ghosts, it's my duty as your best friend to believe you."

"Something's wrong, Murdock," she announced softly while clinging to him. "I can't put my finger on it, but I just have a really bad feeling."

"Whatever's happening, we'll work through it together, Harley," he announced and affectionately hugged her to his side. "I promise."

Chapter Eleven

$\mathcal{T}$he dark night skies indicated an approaching storm. Lightning could be seen in the distance over the ocean. The wind blew harshly as waves fiercely crashed against the cliffs below the hotel. Within the lighthouse lantern room, Harley sat casually reclined on the bench. She held her head in her hand before the glass walls while watching the distant storm. She remained sad and distracted. Murdock entered the lantern room, approached her, and moved her legs to sit alongside her, allowing her legs to rest on his lap. He looked outside to the threatening skies in silence and seemed to stare with her, lost in her same world.

"They're never coming back, are they?" she whispered without taking her eyes off the distant horizon.

"I suppose there's always hope."

"They asked me to go with them," she remarked softly and remained distant. "I just wanted them to have some time alone together. I should have gone with them."

Murdock now stared at her with a sympathetic yet commanding look. "Wishing you were with them doesn't change anything, Harley."

"I know, but at least I wouldn't have to miss them," she replied softly. "I sometimes go through their things stored in the attic and try to remember the good times, but lately, I can't remember any." She fell silent a moment while maintaining her stare. "I'm going to lose the hotel. I can feel three generations shaking their heads with disappointment at me."

"You're not going to lose the hotel," he insisted while gently caressing her legs on his lap. "You'll get that bank loan, and we'll make this place a summer hot spot again, I promise."

Harley finally looked at him and smiled gently. "I don't know what I'd ever do without you."

"Well, you'll never have to find out," he announced cheerfully and attempted a smile. "You're stuck with me forever."

Harley sat forward and moved into his arms. Murdock held her against him, shut his eyes, and held back his sigh.

†

Bernie paced her guestroom while Kaplan relaxed on the bed, his laptop across his legs as he casually tapped on the keyboard. Bernie remained anxious and eyed her husband several times. It was obvious his ability to work quietly and in an enormously relaxed state irritated her.

"Shouldn't we call that real estate woman?" Bernie finally demanded while spinning on her heels to face her husband.

"You know she's entertaining tonight," Kaplan insisted without looking up. "She's not going to answer her phone. Just relax. It'll all work out."

"I can't relax," Bernie snapped and continued her pacing. "Do you have any idea what we could do with this place?"

"Yes, dear," he replied again without looking up, "I'm aware, but even in its current condition, this place is out of our price range." He sighed and set his laptop aside, finally looking at his impatient wife. "We need to let the girl implode in order for the price to drop."

"She's not going to *implode*," Bernie scoffed. "Her fool Murdock won't let that happen. We need to get him out of the picture. That would throw her off her game."

"And how do you propose to get a young man who worships the ground Harley walks upon out of the picture?" Kaplan almost demanded.

"Surely we know some hot girl willing to lure him away," Bernie replied. "Not forever but just long enough to crash Harley's world."

"You may be on to something there," Kaplan replied while sinking into thought. "Certainly better than mine."

"What was your idea?" she asked while cocking her head to the side.

"Frame him for something just big enough to toss him in jail for a month or more," Kaplan replied. "He'd have to spend any money he has left on attorney fees, and he'd lose his credibility to co-sign any bank loan."

Bernie grinned and laughed softly. "You're an evil man, Kaplan."

"Yeah, I make myself proud."

Chapter Twelve

Midnight.   Harley appeared from the corridor past the elevators and walked across the lobby, clearly distracted while tapping on her tablet screen with irritation. Remy remained behind the desk and read her book, offering no assistance to Harley's electronics frustration. Harley tossed her tablet onto the sturdy coffee table with disgust and then cast herself into the plush chair near the large set of windows overlooking the beachside terrace. She stared out the window beyond the terrace toward the distant ocean. She saw someone's reflection as they crossed the lobby. Harley glanced behind her, but there was no one there. Remy remained quietly behind the desk while reading her book, and she hadn't moved from her spot in over an hour. Harley scanned the eerily creepy lobby for any sign of whom she had seen passing through. When she didn't see anyone, she chalked it up to the hotel ghosts roaming their familiar patterns. It was, after all, midnight. The witching hour was upon them. She shivered slightly, having successfully given herself the creeps.

As she looked back out the wall of windows, she saw the reflection of a man dressed in vintage clothing standing a few feet behind her holding a gun. Harley gasped and spun around on her chair as the gun fired, although not nearly as loud as she had anticipated. She held her breath and awaited the sting of a bullet, but the man and his gun were both gone. Harley shifted slightly in her chair, silently cursed out the ghosts, and attempted to relax. Her eyes strayed to the heavy, carved coffee table before her. She stared at what was possibly a bullet hole in the wood that had been there for nearly one hundred years.

Rumor had it the bullet hole came from a gun belonging to one of the three owners during their last stand in the lobby on that fateful evening. It was the same evening that left all three men dead. She was about to look away when she saw blood dripping from the bullet hole in the wood. Harley stared with horror at the dripping blood but refused to react. It was the ghosts messing with her mind. She didn't understand the uptick in paranormal occurrences in recent months. She put the bleeding hole in the coffee table from her mind and resumed staring out the window. She wasn't about to let the ghosts ruin her perfect evening of wallowing in self-pity.

The front door opened to wind and rain, startling both women. Dane and Alicia hurried inside while screaming and laughing at their nearly soaked condition. Harley ignored the happy couple. She wasn't about to let their good mood spoil her bad one. It wasn't that Harley was jealous of Alicia's newly found relationship with a sophisticated, intelligent world traveler turned successful businessman, but it was somewhat annoying that the buxom blond would always get there first. The more she thought about it, the more Harley realized she was jealous of Alicia. She'd love to find someone like Dane. Not nearly as high-strung as Murdock, he had a blissful calm about him. Sadly, he was out of her league both intellectually and in sophistication. Arm candy such as Alicia complimented his lifestyle more than a financially struggling tom girl.

Dane shut the door behind them and flicked water from his drenched hands. Alicia giggled at her soaked body and drenched hair now flattened on her head. Both appeared to be in an amazingly good mood despite being drenched.

"Some freak storm, huh?" Alicia announced while brushing the wet hair from her face.

"Never trust the weather service," Dane replied while laughing at his own soaked clothing.

"How could the sky be so clear in the valley and be storming like a bastard up here?" she asked while giving him a quizzical look through slightly runny mascara.

"Altitude, perhaps."

They headed across the lobby, sloshing the entire way. Remy shut her book as the couple crossed the lobby. She rounded the desk and met them halfway to the elevators.

"Pretty wild weather, huh?" Remy teased while taking in an eyeful of the soaked couple.

"We were just remarking about that," Alicia joked.

"I'm turning in for the night," Remy casually informed them. "If you need anything, the front desk calls will be routed to my room."

"Thanks, Remy," Dane replied.

"We won't need anything, honey," Alicia announced while grinning lustfully as she clung to Dane's arm through his soaked jacket sleeve.

Remy returned a knowing grin then headed down the corridor past the elevators. Alicia clung to Dane's arm despite their wet clothes and smiled lustfully.

"I'm thinking a bubble bath for two."

Dane grinned at the suggestion. "There's still some wine left from last night." He then glanced across the lobby at the wall of windows.

Harley sat in her plush chair looking out the window toward the dark, violent ocean. Dane's expression became less jovial as he stared at the young woman. He looked back at Alicia, offered a pleasant smile, and patted her arm.

"Why don't you start that bath," Dane suggested. "I'll be along in a minute."

Alicia grinned at the suggestion, kissed him quickly on the lips, and then headed for the elevator. Dane approached Harley curled in her chair. She didn't bother looking up and barely acknowledged his presence. He removed his soaked jacket to reveal his less wet clothes beneath and uncertainly sat on the solid wood coffee table before her chair. He studied her troubled expression a moment before speaking.

"Everything okay?" he asked gently.

Harley stared outside without even looking at him. At first, she was reluctant to respond to the question. "We're in for one hell of a storm," she finally remarked softly while remaining preoccupied with the darkness over the ocean.

"I noticed," he replied then tilted his head while studying her. "Do storms bother you?"

"It was a storm much like this that took my parents from me," she almost whispered and felt the familiar ache in her heart.

Dane appeared reluctant to speak, fidgeted slightly, and then asked softly, "What happened?"

Harley inhaled deeply and finally looked at him. "I shouldn't bother you with my problems." She forced a tiny smile. "Sounds like you have a romantic evening ahead of you. I wouldn't want to spoil that for you."

"I have time," he countered.

She held her breath a moment then returned to staring out the window. "My father bought this incredible vintage yacht for their anniversary. *The Dream Catcher.*" She looked at him and managed a smile. "My father was so proud of that yacht." Harley hesitated then drew in a shaken breath. "They went out sailing one afternoon. There was a freak storm, and they were never heard from again." She again looked out the window and drifted off to a different time. "Some nights I stare out at the ocean and swear I see their yacht as they attempt to find their way home." She cast a look at him. "That's why I keep the beacon shining. I want them to know I'm still here waiting for them."

"I'm sure they know."

Harley stared at him a long moment then managed a tiny smile. "You probably shouldn't keep Alicia waiting. The power tends to go out during storms, and the backup generator isn't always reliable," she informed him. "I wouldn't want you getting stuck in the elevator."

Dane looked across the lobby then fidgeted slightly as he looked back at Harley and smiled gently.

"Are you sure you'll be okay?" he asked in a gentle tone. "I don't want to leave you like this. I can stay with you a little while longer."

Harley grinned at his reluctance to leave and laughed softly. "You realize you're risking a sure thing with Alicia with each passing minute."

"I know, but something's compelling me to stay," he replied as his expression suddenly changed. "I can't explain it, but I feel like I should be here."

"You've been out of the dating scene a while, haven't you?" she asked while studying him.

"Longer than I care to admit, but what does that have to do with--?"

"I'm guessing you're having performance jitters," she replied simply. "Don't worry; Alicia will show you the way."

"Your *guess* is a little off base."

"Well, you're certainly not hanging around down here with me because I'm that interesting," she replied. "And no man in his right mind would trade a 'sure thing' for me. Rumor around town puts me somewhere between frigid and a tease." She held back her laugh. "Considering I've been stringing Murdock along since I was fifteen, there's probably some credence to those rumors."

Dane tensed slightly and avoided eye contact. "I assure you, you're selling yourself a little short there. When the right man comes along, he'd certainly prefer you over the sure thing," he remarked then fidgeted. "Besides, I realize I'm much too old for you, and I doubt you're the type to fall for a fat wallet."

"Sounds like you're the one selling yourself short," she replied while eying him and raising her brow.

Dane stared at her a moment, giving the comment some consideration then chuckled softly. "Okay, now you're just messing with me," he announced and stood. "On that note, I'm going upstairs for my 'sure thing'."

Harley grinned. "Go get 'em, stud."

Dane eyed her as he passed and hid his smile. "You are a wicked, wicked girl."

He approached the elevators, pressed the button, and then looked back at Harley, who now leaned over the side of the chair while grinning and gave him a thumbs up. Dane rolled his eyes while hiding his embarrassed smile and ducked inside the elevator as the doors opened. Once Dane disappeared, Harley's smile faded and depression quickly returned. She groaned softly then stood, approached the front desk, and headed behind it to work on the computer. When she typed on the keyboard, nothing happened. She frowned and pounded on the keys.

"Stupid piece of shit!"

Lightning flashed brilliantly, lighting the entire lobby. A loud crack of thunder followed. She looked toward the lobby windows then to the ceiling. The power went out as if on command.

"Right on cue," she moaned softly.

She looked around the dark lobby a moment and waited for the power to come back on. Nothing happened, although she didn't seem too surprised.

"And of course the backup generator doesn't automatically come on like it's supposed to," she muttered. "I wish just one thing worked as it's supposed to around here."

Disgusted, Harley removed a flashlight from beneath the front desk and headed for the long corridor past the elevators.

"I just love that basement in the dark," she scoffed. "Creepy, spider infested junkyard."

✝

*W*ithin the dark elevator, the glow from a cell phone brightened the small area to reveal Dane. He leaned against the wall in the motionless elevator and looked around, although there was nothing to see. He groaned softly while raking his fingers through his wet hair.

"Well, she did try to warn me."

Chapter Thirteen

*H*arley walked through the dark basement by the gleam of her flashlight. The light lent an eerie glow to the strange objects stored within the basement. The image of a man, unbeknownst to her, was present in the shadows as she passed. Harley paused before the large generator, took a moment to glance over the monstrosity, and then pressed a button. Nothing happened. Harley stared at the generator a moment with disbelief. She pressed the button again but still nothing. She pressed the button several more times and cried out with anger.

"Piece of crap!"

She heard a clatter across the basement, causing her to turn quickly. She shined her flashlight across the room, scanning the area. The flashlight created shadows on every wall from the clutter of stored objects. Something moved across the basement, or at least she thought she saw something move. Harley attempted to follow the moving object with her flashlight, but she couldn't locate it. Something then touched her shoulder. She turned with a startled scream and shined the light behind her. There was no one there. She then heard soft voices whispering around her. She again looked around with a startled gasp.

The voices whispered, "en forskyvning I tid; noen er tapt."

Harley looked around, uncertain of what she'd heard. "Is someone there?"

There was no response. A cold breeze blew past her. Harley again jumped and appeared alarmed. It wasn't the first time she'd encountered strange happenings within the basement or the hotel for that matter. She didn't want to believe in ghosts, but they seemed reluctant to abide by her wishes. Being alone in the darkness of the basement with a possible ghostly presence was almost more than she could handle. She hurried across the basement while shining her light all around her as she headed for the stairs.

Once she reached the stairs, she practically ran up them. She hurried past the kitchen. The whispering voices were behind her, almost as if they were following her.

"en forskyvning I tid; noen er tapt."

What were they saying? She wasn't sure she wanted to know. They'd rarely spoken to her before, and she wished they'd return to their silent hauntings. The ghostly voices appeared to be gaining on her, frightening her.

"en forskyvning I tid; neon er tapt," the ghostly voices continued but now closer.

✝

*R*hodes hurried across the hotel's dark office with the blueprints under his shirt. He opened the drawer beneath the secretary and returned the blueprints to their original location. Once he closed the drawer, he leaned against the secretary with his forearm and sank into thought while strumming his fingers. The office door opened, causing Rhodes to jump. As Decker slipped into the office, Rhodes relaxed.

"What are you doing here?" Rhodes softly demanded. "You're supposed to be keeping an eye on Murdock."

"We have a problem," Decker muttered.

Rhodes straightened and stared at his friend through the dim lighting. "What sort of problem?"

"It's Murdock," Decker announced. "He's not in his room."

Rhodes became angry. "You assured me you'd be able to keep an eye on him. He's going to get in the way and ruin everything."

"I'm sorry. I lost track of him," Decker announced sternly. "The guy moves in stealth mode."

"Well, find him," Rhodes demanded, his hostility showing. "Where's Harley?"

"Last time I saw her, she was heading for the basement to start the generator," Decker replied. "She'll be there a while. That generator is one of the cheapest and worst on the market."

"At least one thing is still going according to plan," Rhodes scoffed then glared at his friend. "Go! Find Murdock and keep him busy."

Decker nodded and slipped from the office.

Chapter Fourteen

*H*arley looked behind her as she headed along the corridor for the lobby while attempting to outrun the ghostly voices. She entered the lobby and suddenly collided with someone. Harley screamed in response and whipped her head in the direction of the person before her, shinning her light on him. Rhodes held onto her shoulders to keep her from falling and grinned while chuckling at her mild hysteria. She was glad someone was amused by her fear.

"What's the matter, Harley?" Rhodes teased. "Afraid of the dark?"

Harley took a step back and away from Rhodes to put some distance between them. She attempted to act casual despite her anxieties.

"No, just very big spiders," she informed him while fidgeting. At least her ghostly following had given up their pursuit. Rhodes was good for something after all. "If you'll excuse me, I need to find Murdock to start the backup generator."

She briskly walked past him. The last thing she wanted was to be alone with Rhodes in the dark. Rhodes turned and followed her. She watched him out of the corner of her eye as he kept pace with her. She didn't know why he frightened her the way he did. He was probably harmless, but she always felt he was stalking her, attempting to corner her.

"I can help with the generator," he insisted.

Being alone with Rhodes, in the dark, in the creepy basement was the last thing she wanted or needed. Without looking back at the man following her, she responded, "Thanks, but my insurance company wouldn't approve."

As she continued into the lobby, Harley glanced behind her. Rhodes continued along the corridor in the opposite direction toward the stairs. She was grateful he lost interest and went his own way. From within the darkness, a light suddenly shined in her face, startling her. Harley jumped with surprise and stared at the light blinding her, momentarily frozen by it. The flashlight lowered to reveal Murdock wearing a sly grin on his face.

"You're certainly jumpy," he teased at her expense. "See another ghost?"

"Worse," Harley muttered while attempting to relax and rubbed her chilled arms while darting looks around the dark room. "I ran into Rhodes in the dark."

Murdock's frown resembled a sneer. "You're right, that is worse," he muttered. "Problem with the generator again, or were you too afraid to go down there by yourself?"

"As usual, I couldn't start it."

He shook his head with disgust. "You need to call that salesman back out and have that piece of crap replaced," Murdock informed her in a firm tone.

"It's on my 'to do' list right after buying groceries," she muttered.

"Come on," he announced with a sigh. "Let's have a look at that oversized paperweight."

Harley and Murdock headed back down the hall toward the elevators then on to the basement. She couldn't deny the ghostly voices had her a little more than rattled. Thankfully, she no longer heard them.

"You should let me co-sign for that loan," Murdock informed her. "It'll help push it through faster."

"I'm not taking your money, Murdock," she insisted firmly then muttered, "until I absolutely have to. It's bad enough you work here for free."

"Room and board," he reminded casually. "It pans out in the end."

"With all the groceries you buy, it's hardly panning out for you in the end."

"I'll just put it on your tab," he teased.

"I can't afford your tab as it is."

"That's part of my diabolical plan," he informed her while grinning. "When you think you owe me too much, you'll eventually change your mind and marry me."

She managed a smile and laughed softly. "You're insane, Murdock."

"Yeah, I've been told that for years."

†

$\mathcal{M}$urdock fiddled with a few switches on the generator while Harley held the flashlight. Somehow, the basement seemed less creepy with Murdock by her side. He finished his assessment of the machine then pressed the same button she had. The generator grinded then hummed as if there had never been anything wrong with it. Several emergency lights came on within the basement, causing Harley to look around. Sadly, the basement was almost as creepy in the dim lighting as it had been in the dark. Murdock held his flashlight to his face and laughed evilly, jolting her back from her other world. He lowered the flashlight and grinned.

"You're welcome," he announced cheerfully. "Now you can see those big, hairy spiders when they come for you."

Harley quickly looked at both her shoulders with concern. She could practically feel the imaginary spiders crawling on her, and the thought made her shiver. Murdock pretended to flick one of the imaginary spiders off her shoulder, placed his arm around her, and guided her toward the stairs. Although she felt better with the generator running, she still felt defeat running through her. It was going to be a long, nerve-racking night.

"We're only operating on 20% power with that thing running," she remarked firmly. "The guests won't be happy about that."

"The frat boys and their communal mate are probably half blitzed by now, so I doubt they'll care," he teased. "The only ones left are the spoiled city chick and her pompous husband, and I doubt they're even up at this hour." He then considered his comment. "I wouldn't doubt Dane and Alicia wore each other out by now as well. So we should be good."

66

"Still, I should probably check on our guests," she remarked. "Maybe take them flashlights or something."

"Okay, one quick round of 'howdy dos' then we're both calling it a night," he announced firmly.

"Then the lighthouse beacon--"

"No, Harley," Murdock firmly replied. "I'm not going out there in the pouring rain to start it back up and neither are you."

"Remind me again why there's a backup generator for the lighthouse if we don't intend to use it," she remarked.

"Just because it's there, that doesn't mean I have to go outside and get soaked to start it," Murdock informed her. "Let it go just this once."

She groaned softly and decided to let it go, as he wished.

Chapter Fifteen

*H*arley and Murdock walked along the dimly lit, third floor corridor. All the guests were given rooms with views of the ocean on the third floor, the elevated position providing a better view. Dane was the only one who had been given a room at the opposite end of the floor, providing him some distance from the ongoing frat party. As they headed along the hallway, Murdock was panting being out of breath.

"I don't know why we couldn't take the elevator," he announced. "It's connected to the backup generator."

"And if the generator suddenly stops running, we're stuck in the elevator until someone finds our rotting bodies," she remarked firmly then considered something, which caused her concern. "That reminds me; I should make sure Dane isn't stuck in there."

"If he *was* stranded when the power went out, he'd be safely returned to his floor once the generator kicked in," Murdock remarked then came up with his own thought. "I hadn't thought about that before. Might be fun; us being stuck in an elevator together all night."

Harley glared at Murdock's idea of a good time. He smiled lustfully while suggestively raising his brows. Harley hid her smile and shook her head.

"You need a girlfriend."

He took her hand in his and warmly kissed it. "I'm still holding out for you."

"You're going to be holding out a long time."

"I don't mind," he announced cheerfully and released her hand.

Harley paused before the first occupied room and knocked on Blaine's guestroom door. There was no response, which wasn't too surprising. She knocked a little louder just to be certain the room was empty.

"Blaine, it's Harley," she announced through the closed door. "I brought you a flashlight until the power comes on."

There was still no response, indicating he was probably with his friends elsewhere in the hotel.

"He's either passed out, or he's with the rest of the party animals in one of their rooms," Murdock informed her. "They weren't in the game room. It was empty when I went looking for you."

"We'll try their other guestrooms."

Just as they were about to turn and leave, Harley heard a faint clunk from within Blaine's room. She stopped Murdock and listened by the door. He appeared slightly bewildered by her actions. She knocked a little louder.

"Blaine?"

There was still no response.

"What is it?" Murdock asked while tilting his head with a curious look on his face.

"I heard a sound within the room." She now pounded on the door with urgency. "Blaine, it's Harley. I need to make sure you're okay," she announced firmly. "I'm letting myself in."

Harley unlocked the door with her master key and slowly opened it to reveal the mostly dark, silent room. Harley and Murdock uncertainly entered and paused within the doorway. Murdock flipped the light switch, allowing the sole emergency light to come on. Blaine lie on the floor on the opposite side of the bed near the overturned nightstand. Harley gasped with alarm, hurried toward him, and crouched alongside him.

"Blaine, are you okay?"

Harley struggled to turn him over then immediately gasped with alarm. Blood saturated Blaine's torn white shirt revealing several deep stab wounds. He was still alive! Blaine managed to focus on her, gasped a breath as if about to speak, and then fell limp. Harley released him with a startled gasp, allowing him to fall onto his back. Murdock pulled Harley to her feet while sharing the same horrified expression.

"We need to call the police," Murdock softly cried out while attempting to remain calm but obviously failed.

Harley could barely tear her eyes away from the butchered dead man then looked at her friend. "How?" she suddenly gasped. "The phones are down with the power."

"My cell phone will work."

"On the roof maybe," she announced with panic in her voice. She clutched his arm while staring into his eyes with a serious look. "You need to go get help, Murdock. Drive to the sheriff's office in town."

He was stunned by her insistence. "I'm not leaving you."

"I have to warn the other guests," she softly cried out.

"Are you kidding?" he launched back. "One of your guests is a killer!"

Her mind was racing with a thousand thoughts and scenarios. "We don't know that."

"Yes, we do," he insisted as his eyes widened with horror. "You have one hundred rooms and only six are occupied. This was no random act by some passing stranger." He clutched her shoulders in his hands and stared into her eyes. "You're going to take my car to town and get help. I'll warn your guests when you're safely on your way."

"Murdock--"

"No arguments this time," he now shouted. "You're going!"

Murdock grabbed Harley's arm and pulled her from the room, hurrying her down the corridor and toward the elevator. She protested as he pushed the button.

"No, not the elevator!"

There was no sound from the elevator despite the illuminated light. It was possible the elevator hadn't responded to the recently running generator. One of the nearby guestroom doors opened. Kaplan and Bernie appeared angry as they bolted from their room and approached Harley and Murdock in the hallway.

"What's with the lights?" Kaplan demanded. "I can't see a damned thing in my room."

"We're running on the backup generator," Murdock replied while attempting to keep his cool despite the stress of their current situation.

"How am I supposed to use my laptop?" Kaplan demanded. "Does anything work in this hotel?"

The look on Murdock's face quickly turned hostile. "There's a storm outside, or haven't you noticed," he lashed out with some irritation.

"Murdock--" Harley softly scolded.

"Sorry, Harley," Murdock snarled with insincerity, "manners went out the door three seconds ago."

"I assure you, power is out all over town," Harley informed Kaplan. "It happens during thunderstorms. There's a red outlet in your room that will run electronic devices." She remained tense and fidgeted slightly. "Please, return to your room. We have reason to believe there may be an intruder in the hotel, and we're asking that you remain in your room with the door bolted until the police arrive."

"The police," Bernie shrieked.

Patrice appeared in the hallway from a nearby room and appeared curious as she approached.

"Did someone just mention the police?" Patrice suddenly gasped.

"Yes, there's an intruder in the hotel," Harley informed her. "Please return to your room and keep the door bolted. The police will be here soon."

"I have to tell Blaine," Patrice gasped and attempted to pass them to Blaine's room.

Murdock reacted and swiftly blocked her path. "I can't let you go in there, Patrice."

"What? Why not?" she demanded.

There was an odd silence as Murdock stared at the young woman. Harley cast a glance at her friend and waited for his response. Murdock attempted to compose himself.

"Please, go back to your room and bolt the door," Murdock insisted, maintaining more discipline than Harley thought him capable in an intense situation.

"Did something happen to Blaine?" Patrice suddenly gasped with a look of horror in her eyes.

Harley and Murdock exchanged looks, indicating both were at a loss for the right words. Patrice noticed Harley's hands and appeared alarmed.

"Is that blood?" Patrice suddenly gasped while pointing then became alarmed to the point of hysterical. "Oh, my God! Something happened to Blaine! I have to help him!"

She attempted to bolt past them. Harley caught her by the shoulders and prevented her from passing them.

"He's gone, Patrice," Harley gently but firmly informed her while staring into her panic filled eyes. "I'm sorry, but you need to return to your room and bolt the door."

"Was he murdered?" Kaplan cried out with alarm.

Bernie gasped and placed her hand over her mouth. "Oh, my God!"

It was obvious that Harley and Murdock were quickly losing control of the situation.

"Blaine? Oh, God, no," Patrice cried out and slipped into hysteria. "I have to find Rhodes and Decker!" She pulled free from Harley's grip.

"You can't be running around the hotel in the dark," Harley firmly insisted. "You need to lock yourself in your room. Please do as I say."

"No, I have to find my friends!"

Murdock firmly caught Patrice by the arms and kept her from bolting. He violently forced her to face him. "Listen to me," he shouted in a firm, low voice. "You're going to return to your room and do what Harley says. We'll find your friends, but it's too dangerous to be running around by yourself. Do you understand?" He then glared at Kaplan and Bernie. "Both of you too!"

It seemed as if he'd finally gotten through to all three when the fire alarm suddenly wailed and the firelights flashed. Harley and Murdock exchanged terrified looks. Patrice seized the opportunity and pulled away from Murdock. She ran down the hall before they could stop her.

"Rhodes! Decker!" she cried out while running.

"I need to go after her," Harley insisted.

"That's the fire alarm, Harley," Murdock announced firmly while glaring at her. "You're not going anywhere but out." He turned to the stunned couple and took control of the situation. "Down the stairs--now!"

Murdock forced Harley toward the stairs despite her protests. Kaplan and Bernie hurried after them.

"My laptop!" Kaplan cried out.

"Down those stairs--now!" Murdock ordered while firmly pointing.

"If my laptop is destroyed, I'm suing," Kaplan yelled back.

Murdock released Harley and turned to face Kaplan. He pointed a warning finger in his face while staring him down. "If you don't shut the hell up and get down those stairs, you'll be feeling my fist!"

Bernie grabbed Kaplan's arm and pulled him toward the stairs. Alicia entered the hallway from her room on the opposite end of the floor wearing nothing but a plush hotel bathrobe. Murdock was first to see her, motioning her toward them and the stairs.

"This way, Alicia!"

Alicia looked around with concern then hurried for them and the stairs. Once she passed into the safety of the stairs, Murdock pulled Harley through the door behind Alicia. All five hurried down several flights of stairs then hurried across the lobby. As Murdock attempted to corral the others toward the front door, Harley ran across the lobby toward the desk. She wasted no time leaping over the desk and hurrying for the fire panel. Murdock appeared alarmed then glared at Alicia, Kaplan, and Bernie.

"Go outside and wait in the gazebo," Murdock ordered.

Remy appeared in the corridor from the back of the hotel and hurried toward them. "This way," she announced with a certain calmness about her and motioned them to the front door.

Murdock ran across the lobby toward Harley behind the desk. She scanned the fire panel then looked at him as she grabbed a fire extinguisher from beneath the counter.

"The fire is in the kitchen," she informed him.

"No, Harley," Murdock announced firmly. "The fire department and the police will be here any minute. According to fire protocol, we're supposed to wait outside in the gazebo."

"This hotel is all I have, Murdock," she suddenly cried out. "I can't afford to lose it!"

"Is it worth your life?" he demanded hotly.

"Yes!"

Harley ran for the corridor with the fire extinguisher. Murdock cursed softly, threw his arms in the air with defeat, and ran after her. Remy and Alicia headed for the front doors with Kaplan and Bernie bringing up the rear. When it was obvious no one was paying attention, Kaplan stopped and turned to Bernie.

"I'm going back to the room for my laptop," Kaplan informed her. "You go outside and wait in the gazebo."

"My jewelry," Bernie cried out with alarm. "I'm going with you."

Kaplan and Bernie ran for the elevator and pushed the button. As the doors opened, both jump inside the elevator and disappeared behind the closing doors. The second elevator opened to reveal Dane. He stepped into the lobby and saw Harley and Murdock vanish around the corner. Dane looked around the lobby at the flashing lights and listened to the wailing alarm. Alicia stopped Remy by the front door and motioned to Dane.

"This way!" Alicia cried out.

"Is there a fire?" Dane asked with concern.

"Just another false alarm in the kitchen," Remy casually informed him, appearing calm. "It happens a lot during storms. We'll wait outside in the gazebo for the fire department's 'all clear' just to be safe."

"If you're sure about that, I'll meet you in the gazebo in ten minutes," Dane announced and was about to turn.

"That's not advisable," Remy called after him.

"Dane!" Alicia cried out with concern.

"You need to come with us, Dane," Remy insisted in a stern, authoritative tone.

Dane looked down the corridor, cursed softly, and then reluctantly joined them by the front door.

Chapter Sixteen

*H*arley hurried into the kitchen with the fire extinguisher clutched in her hand. Murdock was only a few steps behind her, attempting to keep up as usual. Both stopped to stare with looks of horror at the massive fire attempting to spread across the back of the kitchen. Murdock sprang into action and grabbed a nearby fire extinguisher as well. Both fought the raging flames, aggressively attacking the nearly out of control fire. Harley hesitated only a moment as she strained to see someone walking across the kitchen near the back door. She was about to call out to the person within the kitchen, when she saw the man covered in blood dragging his bloodied ax. The ax scraped along the tile floor leaving a thin streak of blood alongside his bloodied boot prints. She strained to watch the ghost as he stepped out through the closed, back door. Somehow, the image seemed to hold meaning, but she just didn't know what it meant.

Harley brushed the image from her mind and continued to fight the fire with her extinguisher. Smoke was already filling the large kitchen, making it hard to see let alone breathe. Neither could believe how quickly the fire had spread, considering they hadn't noticed a fire on their way through from the basement. What was more concerning was that the sprinklers hadn't activated. Harley feared the fire would spread to the ceiling and the connecting walls, destroying the entire hotel. Thankfully, it wouldn't take long for the nearby fire department to make it to them on the cliff, but they needed to contain the fire until they arrived to keep the damage to a minimum.

†

*P*atrice ran to the last guestroom door on the right and nearly collided with it from her inability to slow down. She fumbled with her key and unlocked the door. She bolted inside and immediately stopped when she saw Decker rifling through his duffel bag. The door automatically closed behind her.

"We have to find Rhodes and get out of here," she informed Decker in a state near panic.

Decker straightened and gave her a slightly humored look. "Relax," he announced with a chuckle. "It's just a false alarm."

"I'm not talking about the fire alarm," she blurted out. "Blaine is dead."

Decker appeared stunned by her announcement then took two quick steps closer to her and clutched her shoulders. "Are you serious?"

She vigorously nodded. "Harley found him a few minutes ago," Patrice replied. "I think he was murdered, Decker. We have to find Rhodes and get out of here!"

His astonishment to her words only lasted a moment. He searched her eyes and appeared stern. "Fuck Rhodes," he suddenly blurted out. "You and I are out of here."

He grabbed her arm and pulled her toward the door. Decker threw open the door to reveal Rhodes with a look of panic on his face. Patrice and Decker jumped with surprise. Rhodes hurried into the room, appearing shocked and nearly out of breath.

"You won't believe it," Rhodes announced while gasping. "I found Blaine. Someone stabbed him to death! We need to get out of here."

"Tell me you found it," Decker blurted out to his friend.

"Found what?" Patrice suddenly asked.

Rhodes turned to Patrice. "Wait in the hallway for us," he announced. "We'll be along in a minute."

"But--"

"Do as he says, Patrice," Decker ordered.

She obediently did as they ordered and hurried into the hall. Their raised voices could be heard from within the guestroom through the closed door. Patrice paced the small area before the door and waited for her friends. The door finally opened, startling her. She whirled around toward the door as Rhodes left the room. He hurried toward her.

"Decker is grabbing a few things," Rhodes announced while pulling her along the corridor. "We'll wait for him in the parking lot."

Patrice uncertainly nodded and hurried with him toward the elevator. "Shouldn't we take the stairs?"

"The elevator is faster."

Rhodes released her just before the elevator and pressed the down button. Patrice wiped her arm where he had been holding it then pulled back to see blood on her hand. Patrice looked at Rhodes with surprise then eyed his blood-covered hand. Horror swept over her.

"It was you?" she suddenly gasped.

Rhodes frowned with disgust and pulled the bloodied knife from a hidden sheath behind his back. Patrice screamed as he slashed at her with the knife. The first elevator door opened. She lunged into the elevator and repeatedly struck the close door button. Rhodes stuck his arm into the elevator and attempted to slash her between the closing doors. She grabbed his wrist, despite being slashed on the arm, and managed to shove him from the opening. To her relief, the doors closed. Unfortunately, the elevator was heading up rather than down. Patrice held her bleeding arm, sank against the back of the elevator, and sobbed softly.

†

Moments later, the second elevator door opened on the third floor to reveal Kaplan and Bernie. Both hurried from the elevator and for their guestroom just a few doors away. Kaplan unlocked his guestroom door and bolted inside without waiting for his wife to follow. Bernie was about to enter the room behind him when she heard the familiar ding as the first elevator traveling downward arrived on the third floor. She couldn't imagine who would be on the elevator from the fourth floor. Bernie appeared curious and glanced at the elevator. Patrice stepped out of the first elevator looking somewhat dazed and disoriented. Bernie instinctively hurried for Patrice, who remained standing just outside the elevator.

"It's not safe running around on your own, Patrice," Bernie announced. "Stay with us."

As Bernie approached the young woman, she saw Patrice clutching her bleeding throat. A large amount of blood seeped between her fingers and ran down the front of her shirt. Bernie appeared alarmed and stared at the horror-stricken woman drenched in her own blood. Rhodes stepped out of the elevator with the bloodied hunting knife clutched in his hand and a twisted smile on his face. Bernie saw him, gasped, and jumped backwards. Rhodes carelessly shoved the barely standing Patrice aside. She fell to the hallway floor while twitching as the life seeped from her body. Bernie stared with horror at Rhodes. His hands and clothes were now covered in blood, but the psychotic look on his face was far more alarming. Bernie screamed. The nearby guestroom door was thrown open to reveal Kaplan. Bernie ran for him.

"What is--?"

Without explanation, Bernie attempted to push Kaplan for the stairs. Rhodes was suddenly on top of them and slashed his knife at the couple. Bernie screamed and pulled her husband behind her. Kaplan didn't bother to question his wife as he ran in silence with her toward the stairs. Kaplan seemed to be lagging behind, forcing Bernie to pull harder than she should have. His curiosity would be his undoing. Bernie looked back and saw Rhodes pursuing them by only a few feet. Kaplan suddenly fell to his knees, alarming Bernie. As he collapsed to the floor, Bernie saw the knife wound bleeding freely from his lower back. He hadn't been quizzical or simply silent; he'd been stabbed! Bernie screamed and attempted to pull him to his feet as he wheezed. Rhodes was nearly on top of them. Bernie leaped away from Kaplan as Rhodes slashed at her with his knife. She bolted down the hall while screaming despite the chance no one would hear her. She looked back just in time to see Rhodes slashing Kaplan's throat, finishing him off, before running after her.

Chapter Seventeen

*W*ithin the kitchen, the massive fire had nearly engulfed the entire room and was already burning into the ceiling. The smoke was getting thick and Murdock and Harley's efforts were in vain. Murdock tossed his nearly empty fire extinguisher aside and grabbed Harley's arm while glaring at her.

"Time to go, Harley!"

"But--"

"It's too late," he frantically cried out. "We need to get out--now!"

Murdock pulled her toward the corridor. They passed a fire door that had been mysteriously propped open. Bernie was heard screaming from upstairs. Harley suddenly pulled on Murdock's hand clutching her arm and stopped him.

"That's Bernie," Harley cried out. "She's in trouble!"

"Harley, no!"

Harley pulled free from Murdock's grip and bolted up the stairs. Murdock ran after her, swiftly scaling the steps, keeping pace with her. Harley and Murdock heard Bernie's screams coming from the third floor.

"Harley, come on," Murdock cried after her.

"We have to help her!"

They continued up the next flight of stairs and arrived in the third floor corridor. Bernie screamed from within one of the nearby guestrooms beyond the closed door. Harley removed her master key, unlocked the door, and threw it open. Harley and Murdock stood in the open doorway to the guestroom and stared with horror as Bernie crawled across the floor while clutching her bleeding side. Without thinking, Harley ran for Bernie. Murdock suddenly looked to his left. Rhodes slashed at him with the hunting knife, nearly cutting him. Murdock caught his wrist and struggled to keep the knife from slashing him. Rhodes used his large build to toss Murdock from the room. The door closed, automatically locking Murdock outside. Murdock pounded on the door and attempted to open it.

"Harley!"

Harley attempted to pull the bleeding woman to her feet. Bernie looked past her and suddenly screamed. Harley turned to see Rhodes charging for her with the knife clutched in his blood-covered fist. As he thrust downward with the knife, Harley caught his wrist and was nearly driven to her knees by the force. She planted her foot into his abdomen and threw herself backwards. Rhodes was thrown over her and into the glass, balcony doors. The glass doors shattered as Rhodes struck them. Harley grabbed Bernie's arm, pulled her to her feet with amazing strength, and dragged her toward the door. Rhodes was suddenly alongside them and stabbed Bernie, plunging the knife deep into her chest. She screamed and collapsed, nearly taking Harley with her. Murdock continued to pound on the door from the hall.

"Harley!"

Harley jumped back and stared at Rhodes, who stood before her with his bloody knife raised. He slashed at her. Harley leaped out of his path and rolled across the floor. She sprang to her feet, ran for the door, and opened it to reveal Murdock. Rhodes thrust the knife for her back. She saw him out of the corner of her eye and screamed as she bolted away from the door. Before Murdock could enter, the knife struck the doorframe, causing him to jump backwards and fall to the hallway floor. As Rhodes pulled the knife free from the doorframe, the bolt fell across the opening, propping the door open. Rhodes spun around and tackled Harley to the nearby bed, landing on top of her. Harley already had her foot to his abdomen and catapulted him through the broken glass and onto the balcony.

Murdock threw open the door as Harley jumped to her feet not far from the broken balcony doors. She was about to bolt for her friend when Rhodes suddenly grabbed her around the neck. He forcibly slung her out the broken doors and across the balcony with great force, catapulting her over the railing. Harley caught the railing, stopping her deadly fall, and dangled helplessly. Rhodes stepped onto the balcony and raised the knife above Harley, prepared to stab her in the face.

Murdock suddenly appeared behind Rhodes and caught his wrist. Rhodes struggled against Murdock, who held him from behind. Harley looked below her feet where she dangled. There was a small area containing the stone terrace just three stories below. Beyond that was the steep cliff leading down to the jagged rocks before the ocean. Harley gasped and attempted to pull herself up enough to get her feet on the wet balcony ledge. Her foot slipped twice. She looked back into the hotel room. Murdock struggled with Rhodes for control of the knife. Harley lost her grip on the wet railing. As she was about to plummet, her wrist was caught. Harley gasped and looked up. Dane half leaned over the railing while clinging to her wrist and the wet railing. She attempted to grab the vertical rung with her free hand. Rhodes pulled free from Murdock and stabbed him in the shoulder with the knife. Harley witnessed Murdock being thrown backwards while clutching his bleeding shoulder. Horror filled her eyes as she looked back at Dane clinging to her wrist.

"Help Murdock," she cried out.

"I'm not letting go! Give me your other hand," Dane demanded.

"Let me go," she again screamed. "Help Murdock!"

Dane struggled to pull Harley up to safety. She caught the railing and attempted to get her footing while pulling her hand from Dane's.

"Help Murdock," she again screamed from her more secure location.

Both looked behind them into the room. Rhodes was towering over Murdock and plunged the knife into his neck. Murdock gurgled a gasp, spitting up blood, and sank to the floor. Blood poured from his neck wound as Rhodes pulled the knife free. Harley screamed with horror. Her foot suddenly slipped, and she nearly took Dane over the railing with her. Dane struggled again to pull her up. She frantically attempted to get her footing despite the wet balcony. Rhodes approached them with the knife. Harley's eyes widened with horror.

"Behind you!"

Dane looked behind him just as Rhodes plunged down with the bloody knife. Dane attempted to move from his path without releasing Harley's wrist. The knife slashed his arm and across Harley's lower arm. Both cried out in pain. Rhodes pulled back for a second strike.

"Save yourself," Harley screamed.

As the knife plunged downward, Dane released Harley's wrist and swiftly jumped over the railing, joining her on the other side. The knife just barely missed him and struck the railing with a spark and a metallic clang. Dane punched Rhodes in the face, sending him back several feet, buying a few seconds. Dane grabbed Harley around the waist and hoisted her up onto the safety of the railing. Rhodes again lunged for them.

"Down," Dane cried out to her.

Harley ducked on command. Dane clutched the railing with both hands and threw his legs upward. He caught Rhodes around the neck with his legs and flipped him over the railing. Rhodes was catapulted over the balcony, narrowly missing the terrace, and plummeted over the cliff to the rocks below. As Dane landed on the small ledge outside the balcony railing, both stared down at the plummeting man. They couldn't see him land, but both were certain he'd struck the rocks below. Dane climbed over the railing and helped Harley onto the balcony. No sooner had her feet hit the balcony; she released him and ran inside the room to assist Murdock. Harley fell to her knees over Murdock's motionless, blood-soaked body and pulled his head to her chest. He was covered in blood, a pool swiftly collecting on the carpet where he had fallen. Harley clung to her dead friend and sobbed.

Chapter Eighteen

*T*hree days later. What little remained of the fire ravaged kitchen was black with a thick coating of wet soot along the floor, walls, and ceiling. It was difficult to tell it had once been a charming, country kitchen. Although the fire destroyed most of the kitchen, the blaze had been contained, leaving the rest of the hotel intact. Despite being a major renovation, they were fortunate the main structure remained solid and salvageable. It would never be fully restored to its original charm, but the kitchen could be replaced. Those whom had crossed Rhodes' path were gone forever, begging the question, why did he start the fire in the first place? To cover up the murder of his friend? Or had Rhodes simply gone mad? With Rhodes' broken body dragged out to sea, they would never solve the riddle of his psychotic actions.

Within the third floor guestroom, several untouched bloodstains on the carpet became a grisly reminder of the most beloved thing Harley lost that night. Her best friend was gone. A large bloodstain remained within the white taped outline where

Murdock had taken his last breath. Harley sat on the floor alongside the outline where her friend died. She remembered holding her dead friend until the police arrived, but she didn't remember much after that. The last three days were a blur. Harley couldn't even remember if she had left the guestroom, although she was certain the police would have made her leave at some point. She was certain Dane had spent a great deal of time at her side, but she hadn't acknowledged him. She treated Dane poorly and at some point knew she should apologize for her behavior--just not yet. She stared at the large bloodstain in an almost catatonic state. It felt like hours since she'd torn her eyes from the sight. She could still see Murdock lying on the floor, drenched in his own blood, staring off into the afterlife. Was there even an afterlife?

The door opened without the usual electronic hum. The familiar click caused her body to twitch, but she didn't bother looking away from the large bloodstain on the carpet. Had someone entered the room with intent to kill her, she wouldn't resist. Harley hated her dismal thoughts. Murdock wouldn't approve, but she couldn't breathe life back into her own body just yet. Dane uncertainly approached her from behind and stared at her where she sat on the floor.

"I haven't seen you in days," Dane announced gently. "I was starting to worry when I couldn't find you."

She didn't respond or acknowledge him. She heard him. She wanted to respond. He'd been so kind to her, but she just couldn't force any words from her lips. She responded politely to him in her mind, although he couldn't hear it. Dane slowly kneeled alongside her and watched her in silence.

"Is there anything I can do?"

She refused to look at him and drew a deep, shaken breath. Unfortunately, she said the first thing that came to mind. "You should have saved him instead of me."

Dane tensed and subconsciously ran his fingers through his hair. He held his breath a moment while staring at her profile. "I'm not going to apologize for what I did, Harley," he announced firmly. "I made the right decision, and I'd do it again if I had to. I understand survivor's guilt."

"It's not survivor's guilt," she informed him softly without looking back. "I merely exist. Murdock lived. I don't want to exist without him." She hesitated a moment and held her breath. "I've already lost my parents. Pretty soon, I'll lose the hotel as well. I have nothing worth living for."

"Don't talk like that."

"You don't know me, Dane," she informed him softly then hesitated and shut her eyes. "I'm so tired."

She curled up on the floor alongside the tape outline and placed her hand on the center of the bloodstain. She had to force herself to keep from crying. Dane gently placed his hand on her shoulder from behind and leaned closer to her ear where she lie alongside the outline.

"I'll give you one more day to feel sorry for yourself," he gently informed her then turned stern, "but tomorrow morning, you had better be up and doing something productive, or I'll physically remove you from this room."

Dane stood and headed for the door. Harley remained curled on the floor alongside the tape outline while staring at it. She pushed her sorrow aside for only a moment.

"You and Murdock would have been great friends," she announced softly. "He'd be glad you're looking after me."

Dane stopped halfway to the door but didn't look back. He inhaled deeply and stared at the door before him. "Yeah? Well, he'd be disappointed in your behavior."

She knew he was right. "I'll see you in the morning," she replied softly.

He nodded and left the room.

Chapter Nineteen

$\mathcal{I}$t was four o'clock in the morning. The lobby was deathly silent and only a few lights remained on, giving the massive area a creepy feel. Harley wearily shuffled across the lobby wearing one of Murdock's shirts with the sleeves unbuttoned and hanging past her hands. The shirt hung down to her hips, almost covering her frumpy shorts beneath. She clung to her shoulders and remained listless, almost unable to focus on anything. She felt numb, as if every emotion within her suddenly vanished, leaving just a shell. Harley was barely aware that her bare feet were freezing as she walked across the stone floor. Something out of the corner of her eye caught her attention. She looked across the dimly lit lobby to the front desk. Murdock's ghost stood behind the desk as he worked on the computer. Harley stopped and stared at the ghostly image of her friend. He almost seemed real, yet she knew he wasn't. He couldn't be. Could he?

"Murdock?" she gasped softly.

Murdock continued working on the computer without acknowledging her. She practically ran to the front desk and leaned on it across from him. She stared with disbelief at him only a couple of feet from her face. She knew he was a ghost, but he seemed almost alive. She took in every detail of his face as her heart ached for her friend.

"Murdock."

He still didn't acknowledge her. She uncertainly reached out to touch him, but her hand passed through him. There was an odd coldness to the area he occupied, slightly chilling her. Harley continued to stare at him, unable to take her eyes off him. She missed him so much, and now he was standing in front of her once again. Murdock finished working on the computer, walked out from behind the desk, and headed across the lobby. Harley hurried after him. She needed to figure out a way to communicate with him, to get him to notice her. He approached the elevator and vanished through the closed doors. Harley stopped and touched the closed doors with a stunned look.

✝

*D*ane tossed beneath the covers in his guestroom then rolled onto his back with a defeated sigh. He groaned and turned onto his right side while aggressively clutching the pillow, as if balling the pillow up beneath his head would somehow help him sleep. It was obvious for many reasons why sleep was eluding him tonight. He felt an odd chill sweep across his body and opened his eyes. Dane stared at the right side of the bed containing the large amount of blood soaking into the sheets and the top cover. It was now visible to him. He jumped with a startled gasp then flipped onto his left side to reach for the bedside light. He saw Harley sitting on the left side of his bed facing him. She stared at him with a concerned look on her face, almost as if she'd seen a ghost. Dane jumped with surprise while crying out then fell onto his back and groaned softly while clutching his chest. He quickly looked to the right side of the bed in the dim lighting, but the blood was gone. Dane took a moment to shut his eyes and catch his breath from Harley's unannounced visit and his little paranormal escapade. He finally looked at Harley when his breathing wasn't nearly as heavy.

"Damn it, Harley," he gasped softly. "You scared the hell out of me."

Her expression hadn't changed despite nearly giving the man a heart attack. "I saw him," she announced softly with a strange look resembling dread on her face.

Dane gave her a puzzled look. "Who?"

"Murdock."

He stared at her a moment with bewilderment and slowly sat up in bed. "Where?"

"He was a ghost."

He appeared surprised, twitched slightly, and seemed unable to move a moment. "A ghost?" Dane practically gasped then raised his brows. "*You* saw a ghost?"

"I know it sounds insane, but I've felt the presence of ghosts before," she quickly informed him then attempted to remain calm. "This is the first time I've actually seen one. I mean, really seen one. You have to believe me."

Dane stared at her a moment then looked away. He scratched his mussed hair while avoiding looking at her then let out a soft groan.

"I'm not sure I'm capable of having this whole ghost conversation with you right now," he muttered softly.

"I'm sorry," she announced gently while fidgeting. "I never should have woken you like this, it's just--" She again fidgeted while rubbing her arms through the excessively large shirt she wore. "I don't know who else to talk to."

He stared at her a long moment and attempted to process the information despite the early hour. Dane gently smiled, appearing sympathetic.

"No, it's okay, Harley," he reassured her. "I'm here for you. I want you to come to me when things bother you. I don't want you to feel you're alone."

She attempted a tiny smile and fought the urge to cry. "I'm so tired."

"Why don't you try to sleep then?"

She sighed softly and stared at her floppy shorts. "I can't remember the last time I slept," Harley remarked then looked at him and smiled timidly. "Can I lie with you a while?"

Dane appeared stunned by the request as he stared at her with his mouth partially hanging open. Harley saw his expression and suddenly fidgeted.

"I guess that didn't sound good," she remarked and managed a weak smile. "It's just, well, Murdock would let me lie next to him when I couldn't sleep. For some reason I'd sleep great, but he wouldn't."

The comment appeared to take Dane by surprise. He refrained from chuckling and grinned. "Hmm, I wonder why," he remarked then released a soft sigh. "I'm flattered you feel that comfortable around me." He smiled gently. "Of course I don't mind if you want to lie beside me."

Harley felt relieved by his words and wasted little time climbing under the covers with him. She hadn't realized how cold she had been until she felt the warmth beneath the covers. Dane moved over on the queen-sized bed, making room for her, but she followed him across the bed and nestled against him, clinging to his arm. He tensed with surprise to her uninhibited closeness then attempted to relax. Dane fidgeted a moment as he stared at the ceiling then uncertainly looked at the woman nestled against him. Harley was already asleep.

Chapter Twenty

*H*arley tossed slightly beneath the covers within Dane's bed. Her dreams were all over the place. Within her latest nightmare, she walked along the deck of *The Dream Catcher*. The sky was dark and grim as the rain poured down, soaking her. Harley clung to the railing as the ship rode the rough waves. Despite the loud sound of the pouring rain, she could hear her mother screaming from somewhere onboard. She had to find her mother. Harley pulled herself along the railing while attempting to keep from being thrown overboard.

"Mom!"

There was no response, but the storm had reached almost deafening levels that she barely heard her own screams. Harley reached the stern of the ship and saw her mother leaning over the railing while clinging to her father's wrist where he dangled over the opposite side. He was about to slip into the fierce waters below. Harley cried out and ran to help her mother. Although her mother was shouting for her father to hang on and not let go, they weren't speaking any language Harley had known. Her mother was partially pulled over the railing, but she refused to release her husband's hand.

Harley attempted to grab onto her mother while shouting in the same unknown language. She seemed to understand the words at the time. Her hands passed through her mother as if she wasn't even there. Rita was pulled over the railing while still clinging to Rollin. Harley heard her mother scream as she plummeted overboard.

"en forskyvning I tid; noen er tapt," her mother cried out as her voice faded into darkness.

Harley attempted to grab her mother's arm, but her hand passed through her as she plummeted head first after Rollin into the water below. Both vanished before hitting the fierce waves. Harley cried out while straightening. The scenery morphed, and she now stood within the dimly lit third floor guestroom. Harley looked down at the floor and saw Murdock gasping his last breath. She dove to his side, clutched his head to her chest, and sobbed uncontrollably. Harley suddenly woke with a gasp, realizing she was still in Dane's bed, and looked at the man alongside her. Dane slept peacefully on his back just a foot away from her. She moved against him and clung to him as if she'd never let go.

✝

*M*orning came much too fast. Sunlight poked through the part in the curtains, attempting to brighten Dane's guestroom. Dane nestled against Harley from behind while clinging to her beneath the covers. He groaned softly in his sleep and affectionately caressed her hip. Dane nuzzled her neck while gently pressing against her from behind. Despite being mostly asleep, his hand slipped under her shirt and caressed her abdomen while heading for her chest. Harley stopped his traveling hand.

"That's illegal contact, Dane," she remarked gently.

Dane gasped awake with surprise, pulled away, and sat up in bed. He stared at her in the bed alongside him and appeared almost disoriented. He attempted to catch his breath while gently running his fingers through his mussed hair.

"Oh, I'm so sorry," he muttered softly. "I was somewhere else."

Harley laughed softly while rolling onto her back and grinned at him. She thought his boyish embarrassment was adorable. There were many things about Dane she found adorable.

"It's okay. I've come to expect the 'good morning hump'," she informed him without care. "Murdock had his apology down to a science. I'm a good sport about it. Just as long as you're mindful of the hands."

Dane cast a strange look at her then laughed softly while collapsing to the bed. He groaned softly and placed his arm across his eyes.

"Wow, you're a good friend," he remarked with a laugh. "Possibly a little too understanding."

Harley moved against Dane, surprising him with her actions, and clung to his free arm while resting her head on his shoulder. Dane lowered his arm from his face and glanced at the woman nuzzling him.

"Probably why Murdock and I were so close," she announced cheerfully then sank into thought as her smile faded. "He wanted to marry me."

There was an odd silence as Dane stared at her where she remained clinging to him. A warm smile crossed his face as he studied her.

"I'm sure he did."

"I should have accepted," she almost whispered without looking at him. "I didn't know how much I really loved him until a few days ago. I think I put too much importance on attraction." She suddenly lifted her head and looked at Dane. He was still staring at her. "I mean, those feelings would eventually have come, wouldn't they?" She frowned with annoyance at herself. "I should have made him happy. I was being selfish."

"No, Harley. He understood, I promise," Dane gently informed her. "Just because you didn't love him in *that* way, it doesn't alter the fact that you loved him. You two had something very special." He patted her arm wrapped around his arm. "He knew that. I don't think he'd have risked losing that special bond for a physical relationship with you."

She sighed softly and managed a smile while returning to nuzzling his arm. "I wish I could afford to put you on retainer. You have a way of making me feel better."

Dane managed a soft chuckle. "After my behavior this morning, we'll just call it even."

Her mind momentarily strayed to the way he had pressed against her in his sleep. It was almost burned into her mind and merely mentioning it was enough to cause a warm sensation to flood her body. She cast her mildly aroused thoughts aside and shifted with some discomfort.

"We're hardly even," she finally remarked. "You saved my life the other day. I don't know how I'll ever be able to repay you for that." She lifted her eyes and again met his gaze. As he stared back at her, she said the first words that came to her mind. "Maybe my first born."

Dane stared at her a moment with a strange look on his face then finally managed a smile. "Hmm? I'll have to get back to you on that."

Harley managed a laugh, although her mind again strayed back to that brief moment. It was possibly the first time she'd felt alive in months.

Chapter Twenty-one

*L*ater that morning, Harley stood outside the hotel facing the building with a look of horror on her face. Dane exited the hotel through the main entrance, saw her standing on the sidewalk, and uncertainly approached on his way to the nearby parking lot. He paused alongside her, noted the horrified expression on her face, and became curious.

"Harley, are you okay?"

"When did that go up?" she gasped and pointed at the hotel's sign.

Dane looked at the foreclosure sign plastered over the hotel's massive sign. He became tense and avoided looking at her while fidgeting with his car keys.

"I thought you knew," he replied gently. "I mean, I was sure they spoke to your first."

She looked at him as her mouth hung open. "How the hell would I know about that?" she exploded, feeling overwhelmingly irrational. "I mean, the summer season hasn't even started yet. I know we can't open with the fire damage, but certainly the insurance will cover that. They're going to approve the bank loan; I know they are, so how can they do this to me?"

He stared at her with a sad, sympathetic look while fiddling with his keys. "I don't know, Harley," he replied gently and continued to study the now defeated look on her once youthful, attractive face. "Maybe you should call the bank and see if you can straighten this out. I'm sure it's just a misunderstanding." He hesitated and drew a deep, defeated breath. "I'm sure you'll feel better once you speak to someone at the bank."

Harley trembled slightly and placed her hand to her temple. "I can't deal with this, Dane," she nearly gasped and attempted to keep from sobbing in front of him. "I just lost my best friend--and now this!" She nervously looked around, looking for an escape from her world. She felt as if she were about to explode, and she didn't want to show Dane that side of her. "I--I need a drink."

"It's a little early in the morning."

"I don't care."

Harley stormed toward the porch not even sure where she was going then suddenly stopped. For a moment, she didn't move. She inhaled deeply then turned and looked back at Dane with a sympathetic gaze. He hadn't moved and kept his eyes on her. She somehow knew he'd still be there; that wonderful devoted man who belonged to some other woman.

"I'm sorry I'm taking this out on you, Dane," she announced gently and nervously ran her fingers through her hair while shaking her head. "I don't mean to."

"I know. It's okay," he replied then offered a tiny smile. "I have a few things to do at my shop before the grand opening on Saturday. Why don't I bring back some take-out tonight? I'll lend an ear and you can vent all you want this evening."

Harley managed a smile and felt herself nearly down to tears. She wasn't sure how she managed to draw in so many men willing to bring her food. There were days Murdock was the only one standing between her and starvation.

"That's sweet of you," she replied gently, "but I doubt I'll be hungry."

"Nonetheless, I'll bring dinner."

As she stared at him, she didn't want him to leave, not now. She needed his sympathetic shoulder to cry on, but she knew he had his own stress with opening his jewelry store and buying the old mansion across town. Harley needed to be strong and not beg him to stay on her account. Yet, as she stared at him, she was almost certain he'd blow off his entire day if she'd only ask him to. He was a wonderful man, and she'd never put that burden on him. A tiny smile crossed her face.

"Have a nice day at the office, dear," she managed to tease softly, hoping to lighten the mood for his benefit.

Dane smiled and chuckled. "Have fun getting plastered, darling."

Despite his teasing term of endearment, she enjoyed hearing him call her *darling*. She hid her smile and headed into the hotel. As she slowly shut the main door, she watched him head toward his car. He glanced back as if commanded to see that she returned safely inside, but he hadn't seen her staring out the small opening at him. Harley felt a dull pang in her heart. For a brief moment, she almost forgot how much she missed and loved Murdock. She was sad to see Dane leaving even if it was only for a few hours. Harley then realized her grief over Murdock must have been consuming her more than she'd thought. Her overwhelming desire to cling to Dane had to be brought on by her grief. She certainly couldn't be falling for Dane. She'd never allow that to happen. Harley knew she had to give Murdock in death what she never gave him in life; she'd forever be his. It had to be that way.

Harley shut the door, leaned her back against it, and sighed softly. She finally straightened and headed across the lobby, eying the return of the bloodstain in the center of the lobby floor. She was about to put it from her mind and concentrate on finding that bottle of vodka she'd seen once upon a time in her father's office, when she heard a gunshot. Harley jumped and looked around the lobby. She saw the ghostly image of a man, neatly dressed in vintage clothing, falling onto the stone directly over the bloodstain. As soon as his ghostly body struck the stone, he vanished. Within seconds, the bloodstain vanished along with him.

"Okay," she announced with a sigh, "it's officially time to get drunk."

Harley hurried for the main corridor and was about to enter the study when she heard a woman's sharp scream coming from the kitchen. It stopped unnaturally abrupt, alarming her. She was positive it wasn't Remy, so she didn't know whom she had heard nor why she was in the kitchen. She entered the kitchen and paused to look around the severely burned, soot-covered area. It was a dismal reminder of the night that claimed the lives of her guests and her best friend. She didn't see anyone and again wondered if the ghosts were just messing with her mind. It wasn't difficult to do these days.

Since Murdock's death, the hauntings seemed more frequent and had intensified.

Harley turned just in time to see the caretaker swinging the bloodied ax for her. Harley screamed and ducked. His ax passed through her and into the ghostly young maid standing directly behind her. As the ax connected and the maid screamed, both ghosts vanished. Harley held back her gasp and looked around as she slowly straightened from her perceived near death experience. An eerie grinding sound of something metal being dragged across the tile floor echoed through the fire torn kitchen. It was possibly the most chilling sound she'd ever heard. Harley looked across the kitchen toward the terrace door and saw the caretaker and the bloody ax he dragged vanish just within the doorway. Harley's horrified expression said it all. She inhaled a deep shaken breath.

"I'll be outside getting drunk if anyone needs me," she muttered and hurried from the kitchen.

Chapter Twenty-two

*D*ane's jewelry shop was located along Main Street in the center of the small, resort town. The historic building had been one of the first built when the town originally came into existence. The exterior was mostly brick with large windows in the front, now tastefully adorned with decorative bars for added security. Despite being prime time morning, the town was its usual, off-season quiet. Locals greeted one another on the sidewalks, but there weren't many cars driving up and down the well-kept street. Within the jewelry shop, polished glass display cases lined the walls, although the cases remained empty and unlit until closer to the grand opening. Workers were putting the finishing touches on the decorative, crystal chandelier to give the store a wealthy feel. Toward the back of the shop, Dane sat behind a lavish desk and carefully worked on placing diamonds into a white gold bracelet setting.

There was a knock at the door as it opened, being unlocked while the workers were coming and going. Dane immediately looked up, prepared to announce the shop wasn't open yet, and then saw Alicia enter. Dane set the bracelet down and stood as she approached the desk.   As she leaned toward him, he met her halfway and accepted her usual, affectionate quick kiss on the lips.

"I wasn't expecting you this morning," Dane announced then returned to his seat and retrieved the bracelet.

Alicia casually sat on the edge of the desk and watched him immediately return to his work.   She studied him a moment then offered a smile.

"You've been preoccupied lately," she remarked then appeared rigid.   "I was afraid you were avoiding me."

Dane continued his work without looking up despite the comment.   "I have several pieces I need to finish for one of my wealthier customers," he replied and briefly glanced at her while grinning.   "He's marrying a girl young enough to be his granddaughter and wanted to impress her with a million dollars' worth of jewelry for their wedding."

"Impressive," she announced as her eyes lit up.   "It's exciting dating someone so popular."

He grimaced at the comment while working on the bracelet. "I don't feel popular."

Alicia stood, moved behind his chair, and hugged him from behind.   "You are, trust me," she replied proudly then kissed him quickly on the cheek and straightened.   "So how about that romantic evening we've been trying to have for the past week."

He fidgeted slightly and finally looked up at her, although only briefly.   "Oh, yeah," he announced in a timid tone then leaned back in his chair and gave her his full attention.   "I'm sorry about that.   I'm a little overwhelmed tonight."   He fumbled for something to say then forced a smile.   "What about Friday?   We can make another attempt with the hot tub."

"I'll bring the wine this time," she announced gleefully.

"Sounds good," he replied but remained tense.

Alicia removed some papers from her bag, smiled proudly, and placed them on the desk before him.

"They accepted your offer on the house," she announced enthusiastically.   "Congratulations, you're about to own the nicest piece of property in the entire town."

Dane looked at the papers on the desk and appeared surprised.   His expression was hard to read, and he again fumbled with a response.

"With how long they were taking, I thought for sure they intended to turn down the offer," he muttered.

"No, they agreed," she chirped and practically danced while shifting excitedly from foot-to-foot.   "All you need to do is sign the paperwork, and we can set a closing date." She groaned playfully and remained enthusiastic. "I can't wait to get you out of that rat trap of a hotel."

"Rat trap?" he snapped hotly then collected his emotions and managed a smile. "It's rustic and charming."

She cleverly raised her brows, seeming to take his comment as a challenge. "It's falling apart from the foundation up," Alicia boldly remarked then sneered at the thought. "Harley was in way over her head when she turned down that multi-million dollar offer from my client." She groaned softly while shaking her head. "I tried to warn her. Now it's in foreclosure. Someone's going to snap it up at a fraction of its value."

Dane seemed to fidget at the thought then picked up the sales agreement and studied it while slowly leaning back in his chair. He was preoccupied, catching Alicia's attention.

"Correct me if I'm wrong," she announced while attempting a smile to cover her scowl, "but you don't act like a man who suddenly has everything he's ever wanted. I thought you'd be at least a little excited."

"Yeah, me too," he muttered softly while skimming through the contract.

Chapter Twenty-three

As the sun set in the evening, the hotel sat high on the cliff with the lighthouse beacon glistening off the darkening sea. The small, private beach was nearly empty except for a lone woman relaxing on a large, round wicker lounge bed. Harley was casually reclined on the lounge bed nearly halfway into the gentle surf. She stared blankly at the ocean with little regard to the lounge bed being pulled out an inch at a time with the gently lapping waves. Dane removed his socks and shoes at the bottom of the steep, iron steps and approached Harley where she relaxed. He paused alongside her, picked up the empty vodka bottle, and then looked at her with disapproval while raising his brows.

"Have we been drinking all day?"

Harley looked at him while turning onto her stomach and grinned drunkenly. "Well, I don't know about you, but I can safely say I'm feeling no pain."

She rolled onto her back and patted the vacant spot alongside her. Dane shook his head and uncertainly joined her on the lounge bed.

"Careful," he teased with little enthusiasm. "We may end up in England."

"Cheerio, gov'na."

"Well, at least we're in a good mood."

"We are?" she asked with a giggle while slyly raising her brows. "Did *we* get laid tonight?"

"I'm pretty sure Alicia is more than a little annoyed with me at the moment," he replied with a soft groan. "So I can safely say the 'me' part of 'we' did not."

"Nothing a diamond necklace won't cure, I'm sure," Harley teased and giggled. "She's easy to please."

"No," he announced with a dreary sigh. "I'm afraid I won't be buying her forgiveness with expensive gifts."

"Hmm? You've piqued my curiosity," Harley announced and grinned as she clung to the waterproof padding on the lounge bed while studying him. "What ill-conceived act did my favorite archaeologist do to bring about Alicia's wrath?"

"I withdrew my offer on the Foster Estate."

Harley's expression immediately turned serious. She quickly sat up, moved onto her knees, and faced him with a look of astonishment.

"You didn't?" she nearly gasped. "No wonder you're in the doghouse." Harley's eyes widened with horror. "Do you have any idea how much commission you cost her?" Her serious expression suddenly turned humored as she withheld her giggle. "I'm surprised she didn't claw your face off."

"I'm sure she thought about it."

Harley attempted to process the information and hold a moderately intelligent conversation, although it wasn't easy considering how drunk she was. Concern suddenly swept over her as realization set in.

"Did you change your mind about moving here?" she asked almost timidly.

"No, I still intend to live here," he informed her then tensed while staring at her. "I know it's irrational, and I'm probably going to regret it--"

He removed a folded piece of paper from his inner jacket pocket and met Harley's gaze.

"I paid off the loan on your hotel," he replied then sighed softly. "Like it or not, I'm your new partner."

Harley stared at him with astonishment. She wasn't even sure she heard him correctly. She had to be dreaming it. She wanted to respond, but she couldn't find the words. Harley finally blurted out the first thing that came to her mind.

"They're not going to foreclose?" she gasped with surprise. "I get to keep the hotel?"

Dane smiled gently and nodded. "Yes, you get to keep the hotel."

Her heart was pounding so hard, she thought it'd burst through her chest. Excitement swept over her to the heavy burden he'd lifted. She cried out, threw her arms around him, and hugged him while sobbing softly.

"Thank you, Dane," she gasped between sobs. "I don't know how I'll ever repay you."

He timidly returned the embrace, although he appeared to be holding back. A tiny smile crossed his face even though she couldn't see it.

"Well, you can start by finding me more suitable living quarters," he replied matter-of-fact. "Since I officially have no home."

She pulled away, wiped her tears, and laughed softly. "Of course. Anything. You can have the two-bedroom suite next to Murdock's quarters. It used to be my old apartment before I moved into my parents' quarters." She could barely control the smile plastered on her face. "I just can't believe you did that." She groaned and nearly collapsed onto the lounge bed. "We've been struggling to stay afloat since my parents died. You have no idea how much this means to me."

"There is one more catch," he warned.

She laughed softly and waved him off. "Whatever it is, I'm sure it's fine."

"I used all the money I got from the sale of my brown stone in the city to buy off the bank loan on the hotel," he informed her. "There wasn't enough for renovations. This place is going to need some major renovations in order to be successful again."

"I know, but I'm sure we'll get that improvement loan now," she cheerfully informed him. "I mean, we're partners, right? So with both of us on the loan--"

"Actually, there won't be a bank improvement loan. I'm giving up the jewelry store in town and selling off half my inventory to cover the costs of renovations," he replied simply. "That means I'm going to need some space within the hotel to set up shop in order to rebuild my jewelry business."

She stared at him with near horror. She didn't like that he was giving up so much for her. The price to rescue her was too high.

"No, you don't want to sell off your inventory," she gasped as she shook her head then affectionately touched his lower arm. "We'll get the bank loan, I promise."

"The renovations will be more than the current value of the property," he informed her. "I already have a buyer lined up for a substantial portion of my gems. If we do this now, we can have the hotel ready for next summer."

Harley stared at him with mixed emotions. After her parents died, the hotel was always the most important thing in her life, and she let Murdock throw away his future just to keep the hotel afloat. She wasn't sure she wanted another man sacrificing his dreams for hers.

"Are you sure you want to do that?" Harley asked softly while feeling her body twitch at the thought.

"Yeah, I'm sure," he replied then offered a warm smile. "It'll work out. Without the overhead of the shop, I can rebuild my inventory in a year or two."

He seemed confident in his financial decision, allowing her to breathe a sigh of relief. Harley smiled and again hugged him, holding him against her.

"Thank you, Dane," she gasped softly into his neck. "I'll make it up to you, I promise. You won't be sorry."

He returned the embrace and gently nuzzled her head with his. As he held her, the look of doubt showed on his face.

Chapter Twenty-four

*O*ne week later. It was early afternoon as sunlight flooded the rustic lobby. Dane stood behind the front desk while working on the computer as Remy approached with a box containing files. She hoisted it onto the tall counter and groaned, immediately regretting the action. Dane glanced at the box of files then sharply eyed the young woman.

"Did you carry those files all the way from the basement?" he almost demanded. "I would have done that. No need for you to strain yourself."

"Actually, those were in the office," she replied. "That's all the old files I could find." She studied his expression then offered a smile. "Is there anything else I can do?"

Dane handed her a small stack of papers. "Since you offered," he teased then turned serious. "Here are the applications for off-season positions. Most are locals. Would you browse through them and weed out the bad ones? I'm sure you know a lot of the applicants." He casually leaned on the desk and indicated the applications she now held. "We're looking for a full-time groundskeeper, maintenance person, and two housekeepers until the renovations are complete."

Remy gave him a puzzled look. "But I thought you said we're closed until next summer."

"Yes, but we need to keep up with day-to-day maintenance until then," he replied and straightened.

"So what's my work schedule?" Remy asked with a slightly concerned look on her face. "I mean, I've just been filling in around here when there are guests. I still work nights and weekends at the tavern."

"Until we open next summer, your schedule can be flexible, but I'd like you to work full-time weekdays if possible," he replied. "I know you've been filling in for room and board, but this will be a paid position with your room and board included. I'm going to need your help."

She stared at him with her mouth hanging open and a stunned look on her face. "You intend to pay me?" she nearly gasped.

"Well, naturally, I intend to pay you," he replied. "We're going to make this a great vacation spot just as it used to be. The renovations will bring tourists back."

A smile crossed her face. "Well, I certainly can't refuse that offer." She raised the papers cheerfully. "I'll get on these applications right away."

Remy took the applications and hurried across the lobby. Harley passed Remy, who didn't bother acknowledging her. Harley frowned while shaking her head and approached Dane at the desk. She casually leaned on the desk across from him, only briefly glancing at the file box.

"She hasn't talked to me since Murdock died," Harley sadly informed him. "I think she blames me."

"Don't be ridiculous," Dane scolded while staring into her eyes. "It wasn't your fault. No one blames you."

Harley half collapsed on the desk and sank into her dark thoughts. She frowned and eyed Dane. "If I had listened to him when he said we should leave, he wouldn't be dead," she almost whispered.

"Whatever Remy's problem, you shouldn't take it personally. That's on her--not you."

Harley mechanically straightened and forced a smile. "I'm really glad you're here, Dane," she announced gently. "I don't think I could have gotten through any of this without you." Her smile slowly faded. "I'm just sorry it cost you your relationship with Alicia."

He casually waved her off, seemingly unbothered by the comment. "It's not as big of a deal as you want to think," Dane replied. "I knew her two weeks, and we only went out a handful of times. We never even broke the intimacy barrier, which was mostly my fault. I lacked the proper enthusiasm for the relationship." He considered the comment and sighed softly. "There may be something seriously wrong with me."

"I think we're good enough friends now that I can be brutally honest with you," Harley announced simply. "Alicia saw the size of your diamonds and that big commission from that house you didn't buy. She's incapable of seeing what a wonderful man you are, and she doesn't deserve you."

Dane held back his laugh. "I get this funny feeling life with you will be anything but dull."

She grinned proudly and placed her hand on his from across the desk. "I promise to keep you both amused and baffled," Harley teased.

He briefly glanced at her hand on his then placed his free hand over hers and smiled timidly as he stared into her eyes. "I'm counting on that."

Harley gazed into his eyes for a brief moment. She liked what she saw behind his pale blue eyes. Her hand warmly sandwiched between his caused her heartbeat to quicken. Inappropriate thoughts swept through her subconscious, and for a moment, she wondered if he found her half as attractive as she found him. Out of the corner of her eye, she saw someone crossing the lobby and instinctively pulled her hand from his. She cast a look behind her. Harley's smile faded as she saw Murdock's ghost cross the lobby. Dane immediately noted her sudden mood change.

"Something wrong?" Dane asked.

"It's Murdock," she gasped without taking her eyes off her ghostly friend. "Do you see him?"

Dane scanned the lobby in the direction she stared and shook his head. "I'm afraid I don't."

"I'm not crazy," she scoffed and cast a quick glance at him. "I see his ghost, Dane."

"I believe you," he insisted then appeared curious. "Does he see you?"

She continued to watch Murdock. The sight of him was enough to send pangs of guilt throughout her body. How could she even be thinking impure thoughts about Dane? How could she do that to Murdock?

She slowly shook her head in response. "No, I've tried talking to him and even touching him, but he just passes right through me." She then hesitated and glanced back at Dane with noted concern. "I've seen the others too."

"Others?" Dane suddenly asked.

"Bernie, Kaplan, and Patrice."

He stared at her with a look of alarm on his face and uncertainly straightened. "What about *him*?"

"No, thank God," she gasped softly then returned her sights on Murdock's ghost. "I'm going to follow him." She gave a quick wave without looking at Dane. "I'll catch you later."

"Good luck."

Harley hurried across the lobby after Murdock's ghost, afraid she'd lose him again. Dane stared after her and appeared tense. He shook his head, ran his fingers through his hair, and groaned softly

"What have I gotten myself into?"

Chapter Twenty-five

Harley hurried into the kitchen after Murdock and nearly collided with the young maid who died decades ago. Harley gasped with surprise and stepped out of the young ghost's path. She watched the once attractive maid pass on her way to the staff wing. Harley shook the image from her head then looked around the kitchen. Murdock was gone! She had been right behind him, and he still managed to disappear on her. She frowned at her lack of keeping tabs on her ghostly friend, although, it hadn't been her fault. He was, after all, a ghost. Harley then hesitated and looked around the newly remodeled kitchen. It looked almost identical to its original condition but with some modern features. She was pleasantly surprised by the restoration and nodded her approval.

"Huh? What do you know? That was fast," she remarked aloud but to herself.

She heard the clatter of pots and pans. Harley shifted her attention to the island counter and saw the ghost of the plump, older woman wearing a white cook's uniform. Harley sidestepped across the kitchen and watched the woman who had been murdered decades ago. The ghostly cook went about her business and wasn't even aware of Harley's presence, much like Murdock. It seemed with each passing day, the ghosts were becoming more visible and active. Harley wondered if it had anything to do with Murdock's death or her own near death experience. Something was causing increased paranormal activity, but she didn't feel comfortable enough discussing it with Dane or Remy. They would just think she was going insane and possibly attempt to get her therapy.

A strange feeling swept over her. Harley shivered slightly then uncertainly looked toward the nearby fire stairs. The caretaker suddenly walked past her, nearly walking through her. He carried his ax with dried bloodstains covering the blade and handle. She watched him a moment while clinging to her chilled arms as she shivered. He approached the busily working cook by the counter. The older woman never saw him approach. He raised the ax. Harley gasped with horror. The caretaker vanished, allowing the cook to resume with her duties, none the wiser. Harley released her breath and placed her hand to her pounding heart. She then glanced toward the fire stairs.

The night Murdock died was burned into her mind. She could almost hear him begging her to go with him and wait outside. She again heard Patrice's screams. Harley pinched her eyes shut and attempted to wish the sounds from her memory. She once more looked at the fire stairs, hesitated only a moment, and then hurried up them. It was possible Murdock's ghost was returning to the room where he was killed. She didn't know much about ghosts, but she was sure it worked that way.

Harley walked along the third floor corridor and paused outside the infamous guestroom. She drew a deep, shaken breath, reached for the knob, and slowly opened the door. Since the murders, the door's lock had been disabled, so there was no need for her master key. She entered the guestroom and looked around. Her eyes immediately fell to the spot where Murdock had been killed. The stained carpet was gone and had been replaced with all new carpeting. She stared at the spot with surprise that quickly turned to anger.

"You bastard," she growled.

With genuine hostility, Harley whirled around and hurried from the guestroom. She couldn't believe Dane went behind her back and renovated *that* room.

†

*D*ane walked out from behind the lobby desk and nearly collided with Harley. He jumped with surprise, not seeing or hearing her enter the lobby. Harley glared at him with an angry, unpredictable look.

"How could you?" she suddenly lashed out.

Dane stared at her with surprise and appeared uncertain how to respond to her unfounded rage directed at him.

"I'm not sure," he replied almost timidly with limited understanding. "What did I do?"

"You had them renovate the guestroom," she snarled while folding her arms across her chest.

He gave her a bewildered look at the comment. "Which guestroom?"

"*That* guestroom!"

Dane immediately caught her meaning and fumbled for a response. "Oh *that* room," he announced with surprise that quickly turned to concern. "I swear, Harley, I didn't know they were going to renovate that room. I didn't authorize it."

Harley glared at him while maintaining her irritation. Dane uncertainly took a step closer to her and placed his hands on her shoulders.

"I swear, I wouldn't do that," he gently informed her while staring into her hostile eyes. "I would never interfere in your grieving process."

Harley relaxed and allowed her hostility to decrease. She could feel her entire body twitch with anxiety. "I'm sorry," she replied in a softer tone. "I had no right to jump on you like that. I know you'd never purposely do anything to upset me." She fidgeted while insecurely rubbing her arms then smiled more naturally, attempting to lighten the mood. "The kitchen looks good. I'm surprised they finished it so quickly."

Dane stared at her a moment with some bewilderment. "Oh?" he remarked then realized what she'd meant and appeared equally surprised. "I mean, they're done already?" Dane offered a smile and appeared pleased. "Must have been less damage then we'd originally thought." He inhaled deeply and seemed more relaxed. "Listen, I'm going to work on a few pieces of jewelry for some clients. It's going to take a few hours. Why don't you do something fun for a while?"

"I can't remember the last time I had any fun," she remarked then realized how sad and pathetic that sounded.

"Soak in the hot tub, tan on the beach," he announced cheerfully. "Everything here is under control and running smoothly. It's time you stopped worrying about the hotel every minute of the day and let someone else do it for a change."

She gave him a skeptical look then affectionately touched his arm and offered a warm smile. "Are you sure?"

"Yes, I'm positive," he replied while grinning then shook his head. "There aren't any guests to worry about. Take advantage of the peace and quiet."

Harley looked around and considered her options. "Well, maybe I'll sit on the beach a while."

"Excellent idea," he replied cheerfully. "I'll lock up the vodka."

She eyed him sharply then smiled and chuckled softly. "Thanks, Dane."

Harley kissed him quickly but warmly on the lips. She pulled away just as fast, realizing what she'd actually done. Dane stared back at her with some surprise. She smiled with embarrassment by her actions.

"I'll see you later," she announced warmly.

Dane watched Harley head across the lobby for the terrace door. He attempted to hide his grin then shook his head and headed for the main corridor beyond the elevators.

Chapter Twenty-six

*H*arley entered the lighthouse lantern room for her 'alone time', which usually entailed endless sitting and watching for her parents to one day return. She suddenly stopped within the large doorway to see Murdock's ghost standing by the wall of windows staring out to sea. He'd spent many hours hanging out with her in that exact spot. His presence there had to mean something. Perhaps he was waiting for her. Was it possible he was on the other side looking for her as well? She slowly approached and attempted to touch him. Her hand passed through him, leaving her feeling slightly chilled and mostly defeated. Harley allowed feelings of dread sweep over her as she stared at her best friend. It wasn't fair. She could see him, but she couldn't break through enough to communicate with him. He had no idea she was standing alongside him, yet he was undoubtedly looking for her. She needed to find a way to communicate with him, but she didn't know how.

"Murdock?"

He didn't acknowledge her, although she didn't think he would. She leaned against the glass window facing him and watched her friend in silence. His stare remained fixated out the window and into the ocean, staring at nothing in particular. She studied him and his features in great detail. Harley finally folded her arms insecurely across her chest.

"I miss you, Murdock," she announced sadly. "I wish there was something I could do to change what happened. I wish I had the chance to do it over again. I'd do things differently." She hesitated and drew a deep, shaken breath. "I'd give you the relationship you always wanted if you'd only find your way back to me." She felt her body tremble and clung more tightly to her arms. "I know now how much you mean to me."

Despite that he was unaware of her presence; she remained against the window staring at him in silence. Harley gently wiped the tears from her eyes and kept her gaze fixated upon his somber face. She'd remain by his side as long as he stayed within the lantern room.

†

*O*ne o'clock in the morning. Harley entered the nearly silent, dimly lit lobby from the terrace entrance and looked around with confusion. She glanced at the nearby grandfather clock and was in disbelief by the time. How had it gotten to be so late? Had she been outside that long? She looked at her wristwatch to collaborate the correct time, but her watch appeared to be stuck on twelve o'clock. She shook her watch then frowned with annoyance. She hated replacing watch batteries.

"How long was I outside?" she muttered aloud to herself.

It wouldn't be the first time she'd lost track of time and spent hours in the lighthouse. She crossed the lobby, carefully stepping around the large bloodstain that was once again visible. Even when she didn't see it, she usually stepped around it, almost as if fearing it would suck her inside like some mysterious black hole. As she side skirted the bloodstain, she narrowly missed colliding with the ghost of one of the three original owners. She'd seen their pictures in the history book, but she didn't bother placing their names to their faces. The ghost didn't see nor acknowledge her. She watched him as she passed then approached the corridor near the elevators and briefly hesitated.

Decker's ghost had Patrice's ghost pinned against the wall as they kissed passionately while groping one another near the elevator. Seeing the ghostly man and woman together was a chilling reminder of a reality past. The reality was a little too painful. Although she had seen Patrice's ghostly presence since the murders, it was the first time she'd seen Decker's ghost. Was it the late hour bringing out the ghosts of her former guests? While her guests were still alive, she had been convinced the frat party had frequently seeped into the public areas of the hotel when everyone had gone to bed. Seeing them now almost confirmed her suspicions. It was also possible that's why she hadn't seen Decker's ghost before now. Perhaps their haunting patterns took place later at night. The elevator dinged and the doors opened, almost startling her. Rhodes' ghost stepped out from the elevator and walked past her without even acknowledging her. Harley watched with horror on her face as he passed her. She could feel her body twitch with fear and rage at his mere presence. If she hadn't been paralyzed with fear, she'd probably attempt to kill him. Although it would do little good.

A chill rushed past her and then down her spine, causing her to shiver. She watched in silence as Rhodes stopped near Decker and Patrice. He pulled Patrice from Decker's arms and kissed her with unfounded aggression. She returned the kiss and pawed at him with animalistic desire. Harley nervously hurried past them while keeping an eye on all three. Decker didn't remain sidelined long. He pressed against Patrice from behind and groped her while kissing and biting the back of her neck. Harley was almost certain she didn't want to witness what was about to happen in the abandoned hallway. She was just grateful they were unaware of her presence. Harley continued on her way, although she was slightly surprised by what she had just witnessed.

"Wow, you called that one right, Murdock," she muttered softly.

She had assumed Patrice was getting it on with all three guys during their stay, but she didn't believed Murdock's orgy theory. Now she was left with a horrible image burned into her mind and some worse thoughts. Was there any room or surface in the hotel that hadn't been tainted with their sexual acts? As soon as the new maids were brought onboard, she'd want the entire hotel scrubbed and sanitized. A strange chill swept over Harley almost as if she were being followed, forcing her to look back down the hall. Was Rhodes following her? All three ghosts remained by the elevators. Although, when she looked back, she nearly witnessed something else she didn't want to see. Patrice aggressively opened Rhodes belt while pawing and groping him. Before Harley could turn away, Rhodes looked down the corridor in her direction. She swore he made eye contact with her, but he was soon more interested in Patrice's hand slipping inside his pants. Harley hurried down the corridor, wanting to put as much distance between her and Rhodes' ghost as possible. Just in case.

Chapter Twenty-seven

*D*ane's one-bedroom suite, complete with a combination kitchen and living room, had been Harley's living quarters in years past. The suite was located alongside Murdock's suite. Both were across from Harley's new suite, which had belonged to her parents, and Remy's suite. Dane's new quarters were by no means lavish and it was actually rather dated. Dane slept peacefully beneath the covers within his new living quarters on the first floor in the staff wing. He stirred slightly in his sleep and opened his eyes to see Harley comfortably reclined on the bed alongside him while resting against the headboard. Dane jumped with surprise, held back his gasp, and then immediately relaxed.

"You'd think I'd be used to this by now," he muttered then looked at Harley and managed a smile. "Can't sleep?"

"I saw Rhodes," she remarked in a slightly tense tone while remaining uncomfortable.

"Really?" Dane suddenly asked with moderate concern then forced himself to relax. "He was a ghost, I hope."

"If I saw him alive, I wouldn't be sitting here," she firmly informed him as her eyes widened with horror. "I'd be crawling under your skin with you."

Dane smiled sympathetically, pulled the covers back, and patted the bed alongside him. "Come--crawl under my skin. I don't mind."

Harley eagerly slipped under the covers and cuddled against him. There was little reservation this time as he pulled her into his arms and held her against him. She rested her head on his chest and clung to him. As she settled in, Dane subconsciously nuzzled the top of her head with his cheek. He made her feel comfortable even when she felt overly tense. She wanted to compare him with Murdock when she'd curl up against him on those restless nights, but she was painfully aware he wasn't Murdock.

Cuddling with Murdock was almost as if cuddling with herself. He was more of an extension of her own body. With Dane, it felt different. His faint traces of cologne assaulted her senses; his bare legs touching hers created a dull ache within her; and his gently caressing hand on her back sent shockwaves of desire throughout her body. She hated to admit that she was sexually attracted to Dane, which was something she never felt for Murdock. A slight pang of guilt shot through her body. She hated herself for even thinking such a thing.

"Where were you?" Dane finally asked as he held her against him. "I looked everywhere."

"In the lighthouse with Murdock," Harley casually replied while attempting a tiny shrug that caused his hand to brush along her back. She had to admit, she enjoyed the sensation it created. "I guess I lost track of time. My watch stopped."

"I was worried when I couldn't find you."

She lifted her head and met his gaze, her face extremely close to his. Gazing into his blue eyes so close to hers was almost too much to bear. Her eyes strayed to his lips not far from hers. She immediately regretted the action and looked away to keep from kissing him.

She managed a tiny smile that he couldn't see. "It's nice that you worry."

"I'm glad you enjoy my concern," he announced and held back his laugh. "I'm thinking about putting a bell on you, you know, like the kind they put on cats. When I hear the jingle, I'll at least know where to find you."

There was no response. Dane seemed surprise by her lack of comment and looked at her in his arms. She was already asleep. He chuckled softly, gently kissed the top of her head, and nuzzled her with added affection.

"Goodnight, Harley."

†

*E*arly morning. The sun wasn't even up yet, leaving Dane's bedroom mostly dark. Dane clung to Harley from behind; spooning against her while they slept peacefully. He slowly woke with some disorientation, saw her in his arms, smiled, and nuzzled her shoulder. His hand gently caressed her hip and thigh as he subconsciously pressed against her from behind. Once his disorientation passed, Dane released her while groaning and rolled onto his back. He stared at the ceiling with disappointment in himself. Harley turned to face him, nuzzled the pillow, and smiled teasingly.

"Either you broke a record or you're conflicted about something," she announced while grinning.

Dane looked at her with some surprise then shook his head and hid his embarrassment. "Of course you were awake," he muttered softly.

"Ah, conflicted."

Dane leaned on his elbow facing her as well and stared into her eyes. "I don't understand how this was normal behavior for you and Murdock without leading to something more than just friendship," he remarked.

"Probably because I gave him the verbal lashing of a lifetime after the first incident," she teased while grinning.

Dane appeared surprised by the comment. "Then why did you tell me it was okay?"

She shrugged and offered a tiny smile. "Because I like the way you feel against me." Harley hesitated while staring into his eyes. "I don't mind thinking of you in *that* way."

He groaned softly and avoided looking into her eyes at the comment. "You don't know how badly I want to take that the wrong way."

She stared back at him a long moment with a serious expression. "I wish you would," she whispered, somehow unable to control her response.

Dane was momentarily surprised then groaned softly, pulled her against him, and kissed her passionately. To her surprise, Harley returned the passionate kiss with an aggression she never knew possible. She found it difficult to control herself. Any thoughts of Murdock had vanished while she and Dane kissed. Dane firmly ran his hand along her body as he lowered her to the bed. Harley didn't protest or even have second thoughts. She wanted to feel close to Dane. She wanted to feel his body against hers. Perhaps she'd regret it in the morning, but tonight, he was all she wanted.

Chapter Twenty-eight

*W*hile beneath the covers in Dane's bed, Harley twitched in her sleep. Screams within her latest nightmare echoed through her head until she realized the screams were her own. Harley ran along the deck of *The Dream Catcher* in the pouring rain. The ship rocked violently on the rough water in the midst of the violent storm. She attempted to hold onto the railing without slowing her pace, but the deck was slippery. She screamed for her mother and father, but there was no response.

"Harley!" came the familiar male voice yelling for her in a tone that conveyed horror and panic.

"Murdock," she screamed back and hurried along the slippery deck.

She reached the stern and saw Murdock hanging off the back of the ship, clinging to the railing. His hands were slipping on the wet railing. She ran for her friend and caught his wrist. He released the wet railing and grasped her hand. Harley clung to him while crying out and attempted to pull him back onboard. The ship continued to rock violently and the rain pounded against them as they struggled against the storm. The ship shifted violently casting Harley partway over the railing with Murdock. She attempted to hold onto her friend, who now dangled freely over the side. Harley watched helplessly as he was about to be sucked into the waves crashing against the side of the ship. She felt her body slipping on the railing but refused to let go of her friend. Soon she would be taken overboard with him.

"Save yourself," Murdock cried out. "Let go or we both die!"

"No!" she cried out. Harley felt her body slip over the wet railing with her flailing friend. As they plummeted together toward the fierce waves below, she screamed, "en forskyvning I tid; noen er tapt."

Harley's body was suddenly weightless. She awaited the rush of water that would certainly engulf her, but it never came. She breathed easily yet saw only darkness. When Harley opened her eyes, she stood on the balcony of the third floor bedroom overlooking the terrace and the ocean beyond the lighthouse. The world was oddly quiet, and she was somehow at peace.

†

*D*ane slept peacefully on his side beneath the covers within his bed as the early morning sun crept through the part in the curtains. He wearily reached across the bed and felt the empty spot alongside him. He opened his eyes, realized Harley was gone, and looked around the dimly lit room.

"Harley?"

There was no response. Of course, he shouldn't have been surprised. He uncertainly sat up and ran his fingers through his mussed hair.

"Yep," he muttered softly, "definitely getting her a bell." Dane groaned and fell back onto the bed.

†

*T*he massive attic was one large room after another in an endless line of storage areas neatly organized despite the endless

122

number of boxes and furniture. Old living room furniture belonging to Harley's parents had been arranged in a makeshift sitting room of sorts within a large, empty area toward the back of the attic. Harley sat on her father's chair before an antique chest and flipped through her parents' wedding album. She smiled while staring at their wedding pictures. They were so young and full of life. It just wasn't fair that they were taken from her in that way. Sadly, she realized life wasn't fair, and it never would be. Fate was out to get her, or so it seemed. She held back her tears while staring at her parents in the photos.

Chapter Twenty-nine

$\mathcal{I}$t was late evening when Harley stood behind the front desk and again struggled with the computer. Remy didn't offer any support as she stood nearby and looked over several job applications scattered along the desktop. Dane entered the lobby from the back, saw both women at the desk, and approached with some apprehension. Harley looked up as he approached the desk and smiled pleasantly. Remy hadn't realized he'd entered until he was almost in front of the desk.

"Good evening, Dane," Harley announced cheerfully.

Dane gave her a bewildered look but maintained a pleasant smile. "Good evening."

"Hey, Dane," Remy announced while smiling cheerfully and waved the applications. "I'm glad you're here. You'll be happy to know I've narrowed the applicants down to three after the first round of interviews."

Harley glared at her friend with surprise and some annoyance. "What are you talking about?" she almost demanded.

Dane smiled at Remy while attempting to brush off Harley's unfounded irritability. He was obviously bothered by something as well.

"Would you mind going to my desk and checking my planner?" he asked politely of Remy. "See if you can schedule appointments with those three."

"Sure," she chirped cheerfully.

Remy eagerly took the applications and headed for the corridor beyond the elevators. Harley watched her leave with some surprise then looked at Dane.

"What's going on around here?" she suddenly huffed.

"That's what I'd like to know," Dane demanded, becoming annoyed himself while glaring at her impatiently. "Where have you been?"

"Where have I been?" she asked with surprise. "That's a strange question. I've been here at the desk all day. Why do you ask?"

"No, you haven't," he snapped with some irritation. "I've been looking for you for three days. What happened?"

"Three days?" she gasped then turned serious. "Dane, I've been right here. I saw you this morning."

"No, that was three days ago," he informed her. "I woke up and you were gone."

Harley stared at him with a look of surprise as her mouth hung open and appeared unable to respond to the comment. She almost couldn't believe what she was hearing. Dane stared at her stunned expression and was concerned by her reaction.

"Why are you looking at me like that?" he asked.

"I'm not sure what you're implying, but I was never in your bed," she boldly informed him as her eyes widened.

Dane appeared stunned as he stared at her. "You've got to be kidding," he launched with surprise. "Harley, we went at it half the night. How can you not remember?"

His words nearly floored her. She felt the color rise to her cheeks as they burned from the insinuation. Had he actually believed they'd slept together?

"What the hell are you talking about?" she suddenly demanded while feeling her entire body twitch at the mere comment. "You're dating Alicia, remember?"

"Alicia?" he gasped with surprise. "We broke up weeks ago." He suddenly fell silent, studied her a long moment, and then became concerned rather than upset. "What happened, Harley? Why don't you remember any of this?"

"I don't know what medications you're on, Dane, but I think you need to up the dosage," she announced while tensing considerably. She couldn't deny that she had felt a certain attraction toward the man, but after his accusations of sexual involvement, any desire she'd felt was gone. "We should probably call Alicia. She can help you."

"I don't know what's happening to you, Harley, but I want to help," he announced then drew a deep breath while attempting to remain calm. "Why don't we take a walk to the lighthouse? Maybe that will trigger your memory."

She stared at him with horror on her face. "What do you know about the lighthouse?" she gasped with surprise. How did a man she'd just met suddenly know so much about her?

"I know you spend hours in the lantern room staring out into the ocean waiting for your parents to return."

"How do you know that?"

He remained baffled by her question. "You told me."

"I barely know you," she gasped while feeling her entire body trembling. "I wouldn't share that with you."

She was suddenly frightened by Dane's knowledge of her personal information and the unfounded sexual accusations. Something was seriously wrong, and she didn't understand why he was purposely attempting to upset her with his comments. It was possible he was in need of medication, and she debated calling the doctor rather than Alicia.

"Harley, please," he announced gently. "Just listen to me--" Dane attempted to place a sympathetic hand on hers.

She pulled her hand back with a look of concern as if he'd bite. "I think you need to leave," Harley lashed out. "Don't make me call Murdock."

"Murdock?" Dane suddenly gasped with surprise as he stared at her.

"He's very protective of me," she informed him matter-of-fact. "You don't want to piss him off."

He stared at her a long moment with concern and seemed uncertain how to react to the comment. Dane drew a deep breath, groaned softly, and appeared sympathetic.

"I didn't want to do this," he announced gently then hesitated while staring at her. "Harley, you died over a year ago. You and Murdock were killed along with five others when one of your guests turned homicidal."

Harley stared at him with horror then took a step backward and away from him. "What the hell is wrong with you? What sort of sick prank are you pulling?"

He groaned softly with defeat. "You're a ghost, Harley," he gently informed her.

She continued to stare at him with horror then turned angry. "Oh, really?" She slapped him across the face, startling him, and then smirked. "Did that feel like a ghost?"

Although the slap stung, he refrained from reacting. "No, unfortunately for me," he muttered then looked back at her. "I can't explain why I can see and feel you, but I swear I'm the only one who can."

"So you're saying I'm a ghost, but we somehow slept together?" she demanded then sneered at him while folding her arms across her chest. "That's just creepy, and now you're starting to piss me off."

Harley stormed out from behind the desk to get away from the delusional man. Dane caught her arm and stopped her, forcing her to face him. She glared at him with hostility.

"When's the last time Remy spoke to you?" he demanded firmly while raising his brow.

She stared at him with some surprise but quickly covered. "She's mad at me today, but we spoke yesterday," Harley lashed back at him. "I'm not playing this game with you, Dane. You need to let go of my arm, or I *will* hurt you."

"Please, Harley. I can prove it," he informed her. "I just need you to trust me."

Dane was suddenly thrown against the desk with force. He quickly turned and looked at Harley with some surprise. Murdock stood alongside Harley with hostility on his face and pointed a warning finger at Dane.

"Touch her again, and *I'll* hurt you," Murdock proclaimed with a look to back up the threat.

Dane stared at Murdock with horror and confusion. It didn't seem possible!

"It's okay, Murdock," Harley announced while gently patting his shoulder to calm him. "The man's either on drugs or in desperate need of them."

"What's going on?" Murdock demanded without taking his eyes off Dane then finally looked back at Harley. "What did he do to you?"

Harley snorted a soft laugh and indicated Dane with a slight nod. "He's trying to convince me that he and I are lovers," she announced then raised her brows. "Oh, and that I'm a ghost."

Murdock looked from Harley to Dane with astonishment. "That's messed up!"

The expression on Dane's face certainly conveyed his confusion. Murdock took Harley's hand and guided her away without protest toward the terrace doors. Dane watched them with astonishment and slowly shook his head in response.

"I'm not crazy," he announced then took a moment to consider the comment. "I'm almost positive I'm not."

Chapter Thirty

*H*arley sat in the lighthouse lantern room before the large windows while staring out into the ocean. It was a bright, clear night and the sky was filled with stars. She stared into the dark ocean for nearly an hour after her incident with Dane, who had turned into a raving lunatic of sorts. She had a rough day, and she couldn't pretend she wasn't upset by what happened earlier in the lobby. Dane seemed like such a nice guy, so she didn't understand why he'd attempt to lie and deceive her. Trying to convince her she was insane all while attempting to make her believe she'd slept with him was more than she could fathom. She had men come up with creative ways to try to get into her pants before, but she couldn't even guess what Dane's endgame was.

What bothered her most about the whole ordeal was she did find him attractive from the moment they'd met. Under the right circumstances, perhaps he'd be someone she'd consider dating. She didn't understand why some men felt they had to lie their way into a woman's life. It was just a shame, in her opinion. Harley saw

Dane's reflection through the glass as he appeared in the doorway to the lantern room. She rolled her eyes with irritation then stood and turned to face him.

"I don't want to talk to you right now."

Remy appeared in the doorway only a second behind him and looked around the lantern room while rubbing her chilled arms. She seemed genuinely disturbed.

"This place gives me the chills," Remy nearly whispered. "Why did you ask me here?"

"I didn't," Harley snapped.

Neither Dane nor Remy acknowledged Harley's comment. Dane turned to face Remy and took a deep, nervous breath. "I needed to ask you something, and this seemed like the appropriate place, under the circumstances."

"What are you two up to?" Harley demanded while glaring at him with a look that could kill.

Remy approached the windows near Harley, avoided looking at her, and stared out to the ocean. "What did you want to ask me?" Remy asked gently.

Dane drew a deep, tense breath and held it a moment. "Can you tell me what happened the night Harley Brandon died?" he asked almost timidly.

Harley appeared horrified as she stared at Dane then became enraged. She attempted to leave, storming past him. He caught her wrist, stopping her, while keeping his attention on Remy, who slowly turned to face him.

"I don't like to talk about it," Remy replied softly as tears welled in her eyes.

"Don't play along with him, Remy," Harley warned. "I'm not in the mood."

"Please, I have to know," Dane pressed.

Remy inhaled deeply while rubbing her arms. "Last spring, we had six guests. Harley asked me to work that evening, but I was already working at the tavern," she informed him. "The tavern was dead so the bartender said I could leave early, but I didn't want to deal with those guests." Remy frowned then rolled her eyes with disgust. "Two city snobs and the quadruplets from hell. There's not a day that goes by that I'm not burdened with guilt about what happened." She stared at Dane and shook her head. "I should have been here. I should have come back when the bartender told me I could leave. Maybe I could have made a difference." She drew a deep, shaken breath. "And maybe I'd be dead too. Sometimes that's preferable."

Harley stared at Remy with surprise and then concern. Remy wiped the tears from her eyes and sniffed.

"The sheriff told me about the coroner's findings regarding the attack. They found the bodies of five of the guests in various areas around the hotel. The next more violent then the last," she announced and cringed at the thought. Remy then stared off as if in another world. "They found Murdock's blood in one of the third floor guestrooms." She shivered slightly and rubbed her arms. "Harley's blood was on the balcony railing. Traces of the killer's blood was found in both areas." She was silent a moment then drew a deep breath and continued. "They believe Harley was attacked first. When Murdock tried to intervene, the killer went after him. They suspect the killer tossed both their bodies over the balcony and into the ocean. There's some speculation that during the struggle the killer may have gone over the railing with them." She attempted a tiny smile. "I'd like to believe Murdock took the fucker with him."

Dane stared at the heartbroken women in silence as she fought her sorrow. Remy sniffed and again wiped her tears.

"Murdock worshipped the ground Harley walked on," Remy informed him while attempting a smile. "She never knew how lucky she was. I'd been in love with him almost as long as he was in love with her." Her tears started flowing. "Both my friends were taken from me on that forsaken night. I tried to keep the place running for Harley, but with the fire damage, we lost our summer business." She pulled herself together, violently wiped her tears, and inhaled deeply. "You know the rest."

Harley stared at Remy and shared her tears. "My God, I'm dead," she gasped then uncertainly looked at her hands and arms. It just didn't seem possible. She didn't feel dead. It didn't make any sense.

"I know you're hurting, Remy, but I have to tell you something you need to hear," Dane announced gently then drew a nervous breath and reluctantly continued. "I've seen the ghosts of both Harley and Murdock."

Remy stared at Dane with surprise and possible horror. There was no telling how she was going to react to his announcement.

"Is Harley here right now?" Remy suddenly gasped.

"Yes," he replied with some surprise while staring at her and tilted his head. "You actually believe me?"

"Many times I swear I've felt her," she replied softly then smiled warmly. "I'd swear I heard her talking to me--even yelling at me. Sometimes, I felt Murdock. It was comforting. That's why I spent so much time in the lobby and up here. Their presence filled the rooms."

"Yes, they've been both places often."

"Then there were times I felt this horrible feeling of dread," Remy announced with concern and again rubbed her chilled arms. "I'd get this chill--like death's cold fingers on me."

"Rhodes?" Dane asked.

"That's the guy," Remy gasped with horror. "He killed everyone! You really did do your research."

Harley stared at her friend with surprise then looked at Dane, maintaining her disbelief. "It was Rhodes? Why don't I remember any of this?"

Harley pulled away from Dane, despite his attempt to hold her back.

"Where are you going?" Dane almost demanded.

"I'm going to find Murdock, and then we're going to kill Rhodes," Harley replied while glaring at him.

Remy watched Dane with bewilderment at his imaginary conversation. "Are you talking to her?"

Dane stared at Harley and ignored Remy's question. "You can't kill Rhodes, he's dead, remember?"

"I don't care; I'm going to kill him anyway!"

Harley ran from the lantern room while Dane stared helplessly after her. Remy studied Dane in silent question.

He groaned softly and shook his head. "Well, the good news is she finally believes me, but now she wants to kill a man who's already dead," he informed Remy.

"What can we do?" Remy asked.

"I don't know that there's anything we can do." Dane hesitated and sank into his own world. "I've never seen ghosts before, so you can imagine my shock the first time Harley introduced herself to me. For some reason, I can see her, Murdock, and Rhodes but not the other 'guests'. To her, they're real--like Murdock. I just don't understand how I have selective sensory," he muttered while shaking his head. "Why can I see some and not others?" He pondered his question a moment then sighed. "What troubles me most is that I can make physical contact with her and Murdock. They seem almost real to me."

"You mean you can actually touch them?"

"Yeah, I was a little freaked by it at first," he replied. "I nearly jumped out of my skin the first time she talked to me and especially when she touched me." He gently ran his fingers through his hair now uncertain what to do with himself. "What's even more frightening is I actually relived the night of her death with her."

"What? How?" Remy gasped and lunged closer to him, wanting to hear what he had to say. "What happened?"

"You remember that night last month when the power went out and the fire alarm sounded?" he asked while tilting his head. "I went to the kitchen against your advice. That's when I heard her screaming from upstairs and witnessed Rhodes killing Murdock while I was busy saving her."

"You saved her?"

"Yeah, she was about to fall off the balcony," he replied. "I somehow changed the events by tossing the killer over the balcony. Rhodes slashed my arm, and it bled."

"What?"

"Five minutes later the injury vanished, but it was frightening at the time." Dane shivered slightly while reliving the moment. "She's been mourning Murdock's 'death' for a few weeks now. She disappears for days at a time, but for her, it's instantaneous." He hesitated then considered his next comment. "We bonded in more ways then I'm comfortable admitting."

"You slept with Harley? You slept with a ghost?" Remy suddenly gasped then appeared surprised. "Now I'm really confused and possibly concerned. You know she was a virgin when she died, right?"

"Really?" he nearly gasped then shook his head. "No, I didn't know that." He sank into thought but remained bewildered. "That's strange, because she was the aggressor."

"Yeah, that is strange," Remy agreed. "I can understand her roaming the hotel in her old patterns, but I can't believe a ghost is on a learning curve."

"Well, it happened," he replied with a groan. "Right after, she disappeared for three days then came back without any memory of the last couple of weeks. She denied we spent the night together and barely remembers our growing friendship." He gave her a curious look. "What's really troubling is Murdock's ghost suddenly came back to life--so to speak."

"She's looping."

"Looping?"

"Reliving that traumatic event over and over."

"But she's not," he insisted. "She was living an alternate scenario. I changed the events of that night." He shook his head with concern. "None of this makes any sense."

133

Remy appeared to sink into her own thoughts then looked at Dane with a strange realization.

"Maybe it does," she announced. "A long time ago, when we were just teenagers, I remember Harley's father made a strange comment. Something about a curse." Remy stared at him with a strange look. "What if the hotel was cursed? Would that explain all of this?"

"What sort of curse?"

"I don't know. It was just something I overheard," Remy replied. "I just remember it freaked me out for a few weeks. Harley and I speculated that there were ghosts or something even back then. Maybe we were right."

Dane stared at her a long moment with a strange look. "What do you know about Harley's parents?"

"Everything, I suppose."

"Did they speak any language other than English?"

"Why would you ask that? What's that got to do with--?" Remy began but was cut off.

"Did they speak any other language?"

"Spanish maybe," she replied. "I never learned myself. Harley didn't speak it."

"We need to find Harley."

"Why? What are you thinking?" she asked.

He remained deep in thought. "Something unthinkable."

Chapter Thirty-one

*D*ane and Remy walked through the neatly organized attic, which encompassed almost the entire length of the hotel. The items stored within the attic were given greater care than those stored within the cluttered basement. Boxes and furniture were stacked neatly and clearly marked. Dane looked around as Remy led the way along the wide path.

"Why would she be here?" Dane finally asked while looking around.

Remy glanced briefly at him as they continued toward the back of the massive attic. "We stored her parents' things up here after they died," she announced. "Harley would sometimes come up here and look at their wedding album and go through their things. She always believed they'd come back one day."

They approached the neatly contained area set up to resemble a living room despite the wide-open attic surrounding it. Her parents' old sofa and chairs were set up around a coffee table and their end tables and lamps were on either side of the sofa. Harley and Murdock sat close together in silence on the old sofa. Murdock affectionately held Harley, consoling her, while both stared at nothing in their depressed state. Dane saw the couple on the sofa and stopped Remy.

"They're here."

"Murdock too?"

"Yes, they're on the sofa," he announced then indicated where they sat with a slight nod.

Remy stared at the empty sofa as they approached. She slowly sat on the old trunk not far from the coffee table, keeping her eyes on the sofa. Dane sat on the coffee table directly before the couple and studied them a moment. Neither acknowledged him, although he knew they saw him.

"Are you okay?" Dane asked gently.

"Does it matter?" Murdock snapped back while barely glaring at him. "We're dead."

Remy tensed and shifted on the old trunk while staring at the sofa. "Can they hear me?"

Murdock looked at Remy with little emotion. "Of course we can hear you," he muttered.

"She can't hear you, Murdock," Dane informed him. "Only I can see and hear you."

"What did he say?" Remy quickly asked.

"He was just answering you," Dane replied. "They would try to talk to you, but they thought you were ignoring them because you were mad at them."

"No, I'd never be mad at them," Remy immediately protested. "They're my best friends. I wish I could hear them or see them--something."

Murdock stared at Dane and was immediately curious. "Why can you see and hear us? Why not Remy?"

"I'm not sure. I have more questions than answers myself," he replied then looked at Harley, who continued to stare off without looking at him. "I need to ask you some questions about your parents, Harley."

Harley refused to look at him while remaining lost in her own misery. "What about them?" she barely muttered.

"Did they have any old books?"

"Whatever you see here is what they had," she replied with little interest.

"Think, Harley," Dane announced firmly. "This book would be bound in leather, and it would be very old. There would probably be foreign writing on the cover. You'd know it if you saw it."

Harley suddenly looked at him and slowly sat forward despite Murdock's reluctance to let her go.

"My mother's recipe book?" she asked with surprise.

"Is that what she called it?" Dane asked with a curious look. "Her recipe book?"

"Yeah, she said it was in the family for hundreds of years," Harley remarked.

"Can I see it?"

"It wasn't in their apartment," Harley informed him. "Remy, Murdock, and I packed up most all their belongings and brought them up here. I'd remember seeing it."

"I think I would have too," Murdock announced then appeared curious as he sat forward also. "What's so important about an old recipe book?"

"I'm not sure," Dane replied. "We need to find it. If it wasn't in their apartment, where else could it be?"

"The office, but I never saw it there either," Harley informed him.

"If her parents' recipe book was in the kitchen, it's gone now," Remy answered Dane's question, unaware of the responses he was already getting from the couple.

"It would be somewhere safe, perhaps under lock and key; a locked drawer or something with a lock," Dane announced. "Maybe in a secret compartment. Do you remember either of your parents spending an unusual amount of time in one particular place where you weren't allowed?"

Harley and Murdock looked at one another with surprise and realization. Remy, Harley, and Murdock all responded in unison. "The wine cellar."

"It was always locked when we were kids," Remy informed Dane. "Obviously, we were never allowed in there. Rollin was very protective over his wine cellar."

"I went down there once when it wasn't locked. It was the only time her father yelled at me," Murdock informed Dane, remaining curious.

"But I've been in the wine cellar many times since their death," Harley immediately protested then indicated her friends. "We all have. Her recipe book wasn't down there, I assure you. We would have seen it."

"I'm not sure that you would have," Dane replied. "This book would be well hidden and kept safeguarded."

"What's so important about an old recipe book?" Murdock asked with great interest.

"I won't know for sure until I've had a chance to look at it," Dane replied. "We need to find that book."

"Then let's find it," Remy announced boldly. "I'll take you to the wine cellar."

Chapter Thirty-two

*D*ane followed Remy into the almost medieval looking wine cellar, which encompassed the entire twenty-four by twenty-four foot room within the basement. There were racks containing bottles of wine lining all four walls of the stone and wood room. Despite having been in the wine cellar many times in the past, something about the rustic room caused Remy to shiver. Murdock and Harley entered behind them and briefly looked around for any sign of the book. Neither appeared surprised that there wasn't such a book lying around. Apart from the racks of wine lining the walls, the only other objects within the room was an old, no-frills wooden table and two chairs in the center of the wine cellar. Several old, homemade candles were arranged on the table, being mostly burned with large amounts of wax collecting at the stubby brass base. While the other three looked around absolutely certain they'd find nothing, Dane approached the old table and touched the dried wax melted down to the wood.

"The book isn't here, Dane," Remy insisted while rubbing her chilled arms.

Dane didn't respond, seeming more interested in the burned candles. All three looked back at him due to his lack of response. He lit the candles on the table then turned out the lights, leaving them in the now creepy, dimly lit room. All three stared at him with bewildered expressions. He casually sat in one of the two chairs at the table and looked straight ahead. It was unclear what he expected to find, but he was obviously disappointed. Dane frowned and changed seats. He received bewildered looks from the others. Harley studied the odd man a moment longer. Somehow, she found his bizarre behavior almost endearing, yet she was convinced he was just wasting their time.

"What are you doing?" Harley asked while watching him.

"Getting answers."

Remy looked around the room then back at Dane. "I wish I could hear all sides of this conversation," she muttered.

"How do you intend to get answers sitting there?" Murdock demanded becoming impatient.

A strange grin crossed Dane's face. He then nodded to the wine racks across the room from where he sat. "Because I know what questions to ask."

All three looked at the wine rack directly across the room in the direction he faced. Behind the rack, there was a barely visible symbol in fluorescent paint glistening on the wall between the slots. Remy hurried to the rack, looked over it, and then pushed on it. It clicked and popped away from the wall. She jumped with surprise and looked back at Dane. Harley and Murdock appeared stunned to see the rack actually move. Remy slowly pulled the rack away from the dark opening in the stone wall. Dane once again turned on the lights and approached the secret entranceway. He felt around just inside the wall. A light appeared, brightening the room. Dane entered the secret room with the three others following him. All four looked around the strange stone room that looked more like a medieval science lab. There were many burned, homemade candles placed strategically around the room. Old shelves along the right wall contained jars filled with strange powders and plants. The labels were written in some unknown language. An old stone altar was positioned in the center of the room with an antique leather book lying open on top. Harley nearly gasped with horror.

"My parents were Satan worshipers?"

"What is all this stuff?" Remy asked with equal horror while looking around.

"One or both of your parents were witches, Harley," Dane informed her. "This is a witch's spell chamber."

"They were witches?" Remy gasped and looked back at Dane. She took a step back toward the opening to the wine cellar. "Okay, now I'm just freaked."

"You've seen one too many horror movies, Remy," Dane announced reassuringly. "I've studied many cultures, religions, and cults over the years. I've found very little evidence that witches practiced black magic."

Dane approached the altar and casually leafed through the pages in the old book. All three slowly approached and looked over his shoulder.

"What language is that?" Harley asked.

"Norwegian," Dane replied without hesitation.

Murdock groaned while throwing his head back. "Great. Now all we need is a translator."

"You're in luck," Dane replied without looking at him. "I'm fluent in nearly a dozen languages."

Murdock stared at him with a baffled look. "Who the hell are you?" he demanded while placing his hands on his hips. "Who knows a dozen languages?"

Dane shrugged without care. "I've traveled extensively, and I enjoy researching other cultures and languages." He held back his grin. "And, yes, I'm that much of a nerd."

"Okay, so Harley's parents were witches, and Dane is a nerd," Remy remarked nervously, changing the subject as she looked around. "How is that going to help?"

"I just need to find the right passage," Dane informed them while flipping through the old book.

All three watched him with bewildered looks. Dane flipped through several pages, barely skimming each, and finally stopped on one that interested him. He read a moment with great interest then appeared astonished as he looked at Harley. She stared back at him with concern.

"What is it?" she asked as her eyes widened with horror. "What did that book tell you?"

"en forskyvning I tid; noen er tapt."

Harley stared at him with silent surprise at the words she'd heard both in her dreams and from the hotel ghosts.

"A displacement in time; some are lost," Dane translated while staring at her then shook his head with amazement.

"What does that mean?" Murdock almost demanded, losing patience.

Dane continued to stare at Harley and almost laughed. "You're not a ghost."

"But you said--" Harley began then pointed to her friend. "Remy can't see us."

"I know," he remarked while shaking his head. "Somehow, someway, you put a spell on yourself. You're not a ghost; you're a witch."

"Harley's a witch?" Remy gasped with surprise. "How?"

"I don't understand," Harley remarked while staring at the odd man. "Even if I were a witch, how could I put a spell on myself? I've never seen that book before. How would I know what to do or say?"

"I don't really know the answer to that," Dane replied and looked back at the page that interested him. "Maybe your parents taught you that phrase and you suddenly remembered it in a time of crisis."

"I remember hearing it in my dreams," Harley informed him. "I swear, the ghosts were whispering it as well."

"Somehow it stuck," Dane replied.

"Am I a ghost?" Murdock then asked while appearing curious. "I mean, you can see me too, but Remy can't."

"According to the spell that best explains your situation, it happens at a moment of heightened emotion. In Harley's case, confrontation with the death of her friend and her own mortality, this spell would confine the barer to an alternative dimension," Dane informed them then looked at Murdock. "If I'm correct in my translation, Harley removed both of you from the traumatic situation. Not knowing her ability, she wasn't able to reverse the spell."

"Wait," Remy remarked and stared at him with surprise. "So you're saying Harley and Murdock are actually alive and in another dimension?" She gave him a strange look. "And somehow you're able to see into this dimension."

"Yes, that's what I'm saying," Dane replied. "Nothing like this has ever happened to me before. I either have psychic abilities I never knew about, or--"

"Or what?" Remy asked.

He stared at her a moment in silence then drew a deep breath. "Or I share similar DNA," he replied.

"So you're a witch too?" Remy nearly gasped.

"I don't know," Dane replied. "I'm just hypothesizing. When I was a little boy, I was afraid of the dark. To overcome my fears, I had actually convinced myself I was able to create light." He mildly shrugged. "Whether it was real or imagination, I couldn't say."

"Who the hell cares why Dane can see us when no one else can," Murdock launched then looked at Dane with the more important question. "Are you suggesting there's a real possibility that we're not dead?"

"I'd be willing to stake my reputation on that assumption," Dane replied with confidence. "Neither of you are dead. You're just, well, lost."

Murdock and Harley cried out and hugged each other in a brief moment of celebration. They pulled apart and looked at Dane with renewed enthusiasm.

"So if they're stuck in this alternate dimension, how do we get them back?" Remy almost demanded.

"The spell can be broken with the counter spell," Dane replied and offered a tiny smile. "A few simple words and I believe you'll be back from the dead, so to speak."

Harley became enthusiastic and took a step closer to him. She clutched his arm, clinging to him with enthusiastic anticipation. "So what are the words? What do I say?"

His look turned serious as he stared at her. "Before we proceed, Harley, I need to give a word of caution."

"What do you mean?" Murdock suddenly demanded. "Caution about what?"

Harley released Dane's arm while staring at him. She didn't like the sounds of that.

"If I'm correct about the power of the spell and Murdock's status within your spell," he began then hesitated while casting concerned looks at both. "There's the very real possibility someone else was pulled into the spell as well."

All three stared at Dane with bewilderment, not understanding what he was getting at.

Harley's eyes suddenly widened then she gasped, "Rhodes?"

Dane nodded. "Yes, it's very possible Rhodes is living in that dimension with you," he informed her. "I can see you and Murdock, but I can also see Rhodes. I couldn't see the other guests with which you claimed you were interacting. Somehow you were linked to the spiritual world in your dimension." He inhaled deeply while staring into her eyes. "I can't guarantee you won't bring Rhodes back to the real world with you. The specifics are very fuzzy."

"We have to risk it," Harley announced while fidgeting. "I want our lives back."

"I know, but there could be some danger," Dane gently insisted while staring into her eyes. "You need to be prepared for whatever might happen."

"Not to interrupt this conversation that I'm only hearing one side of," Remy announced firmly, "but what if we armed ourselves, so you and I can take out Rhodes if he returns."

"Arming ourselves is an excellent idea, but we don't know where and when they'll return," Dane informed Remy. "I don't know how this works. I don't know that Harley and Murdock will return to their mortal selves here, where they originally vanished, or somewhere else altogether. Same goes for Rhodes."

"What's this 'when' business?" Murdock asked with concern as his eyes widened.

"I don't know if you'll return here and now, or if you'll simply resume where you left off a year ago."

"You mean there's the possibility we could return to Rhodes killing Murdock?" Harley gasped while staring at Dane with horror in her eyes. She couldn't hide her fear but hostility quickly overtook her. "That would make for a crappy spell."

"There's a very real possibility," Dane informed them. "We need to consider all possibilities."

Harley looked at Murdock. The exchange between them was intense. Murdock then appeared sympathetic and released a nervous breath.

"I'm willing to risk it, Harley."

Harley looked at Dane with conviction and released a nervous sigh. "We're in. What's the spell?"

"I'll write it down," Dane informed them. "Wait for me in the lobby. I need to get something from my room."

"What do you need from your room?" Remy asked.

"A little self-preservation insurance," Dane replied. "I believe the occasion calls for it."

Chapter Thirty-three

*D*ane walked along the staff wing corridor while skimming through the pages of the leather bound book as he headed for his quarters. Something caught his attention on one of the pages. He stopped and read the passage with great interest. Dane lifted his eyes from the book and saw Rhodes standing directly in front of him, also eyeing the book. Dane jumped with surprise, although he should have been used to the stealthy coming and goings of those in Harley's dimension.

Rhodes met his gaze and grinned. "What you got there, Dane?"

Dane casually shut the book and kept a disinterested appearance. "It's a book on the history of town," he easily lied. "I found it in the lobby. You can borrow it when I'm finished, if you're into local history."

"Actually, I am," Rhodes announced and again eyed the book. "When will you be finished reading it? I think I'd like to have a look at it."

"I'll probably finish it tonight," Dane informed him while attempting to sound casual. "I can leave it on the coffee table in the lobby for you when I'm done."

"Hey, thanks," Rhodes replied, offered a chilling grin, and then continued down the hallway.

As Rhodes left, Dane glanced around the staff wing corridor with a slightly baffled look. The fact that Rhodes had been in the staff wing was odd in itself. Dane watched him round the corner toward the main guest areas then silently followed him from a distance. He paused by the connecting hallway and peered around the corner. Rhodes entered the nearby lounge. Dane hurried after him and stopped just outside the doorway. He leaned against the wall and pretended to read the book as he listened to the conversation between Rhodes and another man within the lounge. Dane didn't recognize the second voice. Within the empty lounge, Rhodes leaned against the bar near Blaine.

"I can't believe there's no alcohol in this place," Blaine complained. "I mean, it's a bar."

"What do you expect, Blaine? They lost their liquor license a while back," Rhodes informed him then smirked while chuckling. "An unfortunate accident."

"Yeah, I'll bet," Blaine muttered.

Dane remained outside the lounge and appeared slightly stunned that he'd heard another man's voice. Despite confirmation of other ghosts from Rhodes' party, Dane had never seen or heard them before.

"Blaine?" Dane muttered with surprise. "How am I hearing Blaine? It doesn't make sense."

Within the lounge, Blaine eyed his friend then chuckled. "One of *your* unfortunate accidents?"

"Sometimes fate needs a little push in the right direction," Rhodes replied while grinning.

Within the hallway, Dane tilted his head, now curious by the comment. He resisted peering around the corner, fearing they'd catch him listening to them while they conspired. Dane had only had interactions with Rhodes, Harley, and Murdock, although he had been aware that Harley and Murdock interacted with other 'guests' whom he couldn't see or hear. From what he was hearing in Rhodes' own words, it sounded as if Rhodes had been at the hotel prior to the visit that destroyed Harley's world.

"We're not any closer to finding the treasure than we were when we got here," Blaine remarked. "We're running out of time. Patrice is also becoming suspicious. Decker and I can only exclude her for so long."

"Just keep Patrice out of this for one more night," Rhodes firmly insisted. "It won't be long now. I have a plan for us to get our hands on that treasure and a little surprise for Harley." He offered his friend a sinister grin. "Trust me, after tonight; she'll be begging my father to take this property off her hands at a fraction of its value."

"You sound awfully confident."

"I get what I want, Blaine," Rhodes announced. "This hotel will be mine, and then we'll tear the place apart until we find that treasure."

"How do you even know the treasure is in the hotel?" Blaine demanded. "How can you be so sure someone hadn't found it years ago?"

"I have it on good authority," Rhodes informed him while grinning.

"Whose authority?"

"Let's just say one of the original sailors who built this place let it slip during my family's visit here last year," Rhodes informed him.

"Ghosts again?" Blaine demanded. "We're putting all our stock into your delusion of ghosts?"

"I've always been able to see ghosts, you know I have," Rhodes growled with annoyance at his friend's disbelieving comment. "I put a lot of effort into sabotaging this hotel so my father could buy it for me."

"Including selling the owners that vintage yacht?" Blaine scoffed.

"You mean the yacht *you* sold them," Rhodes retorted and cleverly raised his brows.

Blaine stared at Rhodes with surprise. "Did you sabotage that yacht? I didn't sign up for harming anyone. Is that what happened to Harley's parents?"

"No, of course not," Rhodes growled. "I didn't do a damned thing to that yacht. Purely an act of nature. And you just keep your mouth shut about our little deal. If anyone comes back at us about that, you'll look just as guilty."

Both men headed for the lounge doorway. From where he stood in the hallway alongside the doorway, Dane had to react quickly before he was caught. He silently shut the book and hurried back down the corridor toward the kitchen, which would provide the nearest cover. Dane hurried into the kitchen and immediately stopped. The cook from decades past cheerfully mixed cake batter in a bowl while humming softly to herself. Someone moved past Dane, causing him to jump with surprise. He watched as the caretaker walked past him and headed for the back terrace door. The ghosts didn't interact or even acknowledge one another. They just went about their business.

"What is going on?" Dane suddenly muttered while studying the ghosts roaming around the kitchen. "Why can I suddenly see them?"

The fire stairs doorway opened to reveal the ghost of Patrice. She scampered carefree across the kitchen then stopped when she saw Dane. He was slightly alarmed that the unfamiliar female ghost acknowledged him. A grin crossed Patrice's face as she approached him. Dane clutched the book and watched the scantily clad dressed woman as she practically moved against him. He knew who she was without an introduction. He knew she had to be Patrice, from Rhodes' party.

"I haven't seen you around here before," Patrice announced with a giggle while invading his personal space. "Did you just check in?"

"Uh," Dane fumbled while staring at her, uncertain how to respond. "Uh, yes, I did."

"Great," she cooed and placed her hands on his shoulders while moving closer to him. "Maybe you'd like to party with me and my friends later."

He managed a nervous smile and gently brushed her hands from his shoulders.

"It's been a long day," he announced almost timidly. "I'll probably be turning in early."

Patrice took a step back but maintained her grin. "Well, then maybe tomorrow." She gave a lively spin on the balls of her feet and headed across the kitchen.

Dane watched the young woman pass through the ghostly cook. Despite being a ghost herself, Patrice was unaware of the cook's presence. Dane stared with surprise and uncertainty at what was happening. Something was wrong.

"What possibly changed?" he muttered softly while frantically searching for an answer to his new ability to see the hotel ghosts. He then glanced at the book he held and considered something he hadn't before. "The words," Dane gasped softly with realization. "Is it possible I could have performed the spell as a mortal?" He fidgeted slightly at the obvious answer then groaned softly. "Ah, hell no." He frantically flipped through the book, found nothing of interest, and then slammed it shut. He inhaled deeply while sinking into thought. "Is it possible I placed myself in their world with that spell? Or did I somehow pull them from theirs?"

He didn't appear to care for either possibility. Harley needed to end the spell and stop the madness. Dane hurried from the kitchen.

Chapter Thirty-four

Remy stood in the lobby with a fire ax on the desk near her. She eyed the ax several times and appeared nervous, as if waiting for something to happen. Although she was unaware of their presence, Harley and Murdock nervously paced several feet away from her, crossing paths and exchanging worried glances. If Harley wrenched her fingers together any harder, she'd cause herself physical pain. Dane had left them to get something from his room over twenty minutes ago, and his lengthy absence was making everyone nervous. Dane finally appeared within the corridor and passed the elevators. He cocked a semiautomatic, causing all three to jump and look at him as he approached.

"Okay, now I'm ready," Dane announced.

Remy stared at the gun he held and seemed stunned. "Where did you get that?" she gasped.

"I bought it when I chose a career in diamonds," Dane replied then looked at Harley. "I ran into your friend in the staff wing."

"Rhodes?" Harley gasped then shivered. "What was he doing in the staff wing?"

"I had wondered the same thing myself. I overheard him talking with one of his friends," Dane announced and cocked his head slightly. "I think I found the motive for murder."

All three looked at Dane with surprise.

"Apparently, Rhodes tried to buy the hotel after your parents died," Dane continued. "He seems to think the original owners hid the remaining gold coins somewhere within the hotel. Rhodes and his friends were looking for the gold the entire time. I guess when they don't find it Rhodes goes with plan 'b'. Destroy your business and buy it for a fraction of its value."

"Then something went wrong," Harley scoffed while folding her arms across her chest. "He turned on his friends and anyone else who got in the way, huh?"

"That's my guess," Dane replied then glanced at the back corridor. "We should probably get this party started before he comes back this way."

Harley nodded, sharing his concern for a potential interruption. She just wanted to break the spell and return to her life, if possible. Dane looked past Harley to the far end of the lobby. He saw three male ghosts suavely dressed in severely outdated clothing from over one hundred years ago. The three ghost sailors seemed to be having a little meeting near the fireplace. None of the three acknowledged any of them. They were unaware of their presence. It seemed odd that even Harley was unaware of the ghostly men by the fireplace. This time around, Dane appeared to be the only one able to see them.

Dane drew a deep breath and looked back at Harley. "Whenever you're ready."

Harley and Murdock exchanged looks. He took her hand, held it tight, and offered a tiny smile. She attempted to return the smile, but she was too nervous to give her smile any credence. Harley closed her eyes and recited the carefully memorized phrase in Norwegian. Dane and Murdock stared at her with matching looks of concern. Remy stared in the direction Dane stared, although seeing no one and unable to hear Harley's words. None knew what to expect once the spell was broken. Dane's attention suddenly shifted to the ghostly men by the fireplace. A hostile Walter kicked the old, wood carved coffee table. Despite the hard kick, the coffee table barely budged. Dane eyed the coffee table with a curious look.

As Harley finished speaking the words, she felt a strange tingling throughout her body and heard a loud ringing in her ears, blocking out any other sounds. Although she tried, she could no longer feel Murdock's hand holding hers. As the ringing sound faded, she heard voices around her.

t

*S*pring. One year ago. Harley slowly opened her eyes and realized she stood behind the front check-in desk as Bernie chattered endlessly from the opposite side. For a moment, Harley felt awkward and uncertain of her surroundings, almost as if she had dozed off in the middle of Bernie's tirade. Harley looked around the lobby, feeling as if something was wrong. She felt as if she was supposed to be doing something, something urgent, but she didn't know what. Bernie fell silent from her endless chattering and stared at Harley, almost offended by her sudden lack of interest.

"Have you heard a word I've said?" Bernie demanded with annoyance.

"Uh, no. I'm sorry," Harley announced while fidgeting then looked back at Bernie and attempted a smile. "What were you saying?"

"The water pressure in my shower is simply horrible," she announced firmly. "Will you have that handyman of yours look at it again?"

"Uh, sure," Harley replied.

She suddenly felt a strange chill running down her back. Something was off, but she couldn't place it. It almost felt as if she should be somewhere else. What was so urgent? What was commanding her to be somewhere else? Where was she supposed to be other than behind the front desk? Her heart was racing for some odd reason, and her mind wouldn't slow down. Thoughts and images flashed through her head in a flood of emotion that she didn't understand. She was feeling *afraid*. Afraid of what?

"And what's with the cell phone reception around here?" Bernie demanded while continuing with her rant. "I can't get a decent signal anywhere."

Harley forced herself out of her mild trance and focused her attention on the woman before her. "The roof is the only place in the entire resort that has somewhat reliable cell phone reception," Harley reminded her, finally returning to life. "Depending upon weather, even that can be spotty at times."

"Backwoods towns--" Bernie scoffed then walked away from the desk and headed toward the elevators.

Harley again looked around the lobby and sank deep into thought. She felt as if she were in a fog. "What was I doing?" she whispered, feeling oddly puzzled.

Murdock approached the desk with a grin on his face, looking pleased with himself. "You won't believe what I saw in Patrice's room when I was unclogging the shower drain."

Harley managed a smile when she saw her friend. She knew she'd just seen him an hour ago, but somehow she missed him as if he'd been gone a long time. She resisted the urge to throw her arms around him and hug him.

"I'm sure I would," she teased while leaning on the desk. "What did you find?"

"Let's just say it's battery powered and waterproof," he announced while grinning and raising his brows suggestively. He added a throaty chuckle for his own amusement.

"That proves she's not servicing all three of those men. It's physically impossible," Harley informed him with a teasing smile. She suddenly hesitated and considered her comment. Why did she suddenly doubt her own theory?

Murdock studied her distant expression and became curious. "What's that look?"

She looked back at him with a dumbfounded expression then slowly shook her head. "I just had this overwhelming feeling of deja vu," Harley remarked softly. She brushed her feelings aside and attempted to relax, but it wasn't easy.

Murdock glanced with bewilderment across the lobby then looked back at Harley. "I thought Remy was working tonight," he remarked.

"No, she had to work at the tavern," Harley replied. "It's just you and me babysitting."

"Yeah, it certainly feels that way," Murdock muttered. "I'll need to keep happy hips from having sex with one of her lovers in the hot tub again."

"You're terrible," Harley scolded then seemed to remember something. "Oh, uh, Bernie says her shower water pressure is poor. Can you look at that?"

"Sure, but there's nothing I can do about it," he casually replied while leaning on the desk. "It's all in her head."

"Do what you can, okay?"

"You've got it."

Murdock strummed his palms on the desk while grinning then turned to leave.

"Murdock," Harley suddenly gasped and nearly jumped over the desk while staring after him.

He turned and glanced back at her with a slightly startled look. Harley fidgeted while feeling her body tense. She hadn't understood her urgent outburst.

"Uh, look out for yourself, okay," she announced softly as a chill swept across her.

He maintained his baffled look, raised his brows, and then grinned. "I don't know what you have stashed behind that desk, but save me a shot, okay?"

As Murdock headed for the elevators, Harley stared after him and shivered slightly. She then heard the low rumbling of thunder in the near distance, causing her to jump with surprise. Harley looked toward the wall of windows just before the terrace then sank into thought. She uncertainly looked around and again rubbed her chilled shoulders. An overwhelming feeling a dread swept over her, and it was frightening.

✝

$\mathcal{T}$he local tavern located just on the edge of town was a short drive from the hotel on the cliffs. There were few vehicles parked outside the tavern. The tavern was usually swarming with locals on the weekend, but tonight it was nearly empty. The burly bartender leaned on the bar while doing crossword puzzles and appeared completely bored. Remy sat at the bar doodling on her notepad. Her doodle resembled the hotel on the cliff. The drawing wasn't half bad. The bartender finally glanced at his watch then Remy.

"You know, you could leave if you wanted," he informed her. "We're not going to do much business tonight. Half the town is tailgating after that football game in the next county."

Remy gave him a look and snorted a soft laugh. "If it's all the same, I'd rather stay here," she muttered.

"Why?"

She groaned softly and leaned back on her bar stool. "The guests at the hotel are making me insane," Remy informed him. "One couple does nothing but complain, and the party animals are beyond creepy."

The bartender laughed softly. "So you're going to hide here until closing?"

"That's the plan," she announced while returning to her doodling. "I just need one night away, that's all. One night without me isn't going to kill Murdock and Harley."

Remy doodled a moment longer then sat straight and stared at the strange clouds she drew over the hotel. They looked oddly like a butcher knife aimed at the hotel. She stared at the drawing a long moment and appeared anxious. Remy uncertainly glanced around with a look of dread in her eyes and then suddenly rubbed her chilled shoulders. The bartender watched her and appeared curious.

"Is something wrong?"

"No, it's just--" Remy again looked at the strange doodle on her pad. "I feel like I'm supposed to be doing something."

"Does it involve sweeping?" the bartender teased.

Remy glared at him.

Chapter Thirty-five

*T*he extravagant formal party filled the large, expensive city penthouse apartment on the twentieth floor. There were over one hundred well-dressed men and women enjoying free cocktails and the company of other wealthy elites. Dane, looking dashing in his expensive suit, stood near the balcony doors with a drink in his hand and stared out into the dark and stormy night from the elevated position of the penthouse. A distinguished looking man in his forties, Collin, approached with two attractive women wearing skimpy evening gowns. Jasmine and Candy were each attached to his arms. Collin obviously disapproved of his friend standing idle by the large window and staring outside.

"This is a party, Dane," Collin boldly announced. "You're supposed to be mingling."

Dane returned to reality, turning to see the two attractive women linked onto his friend's arms, and immediately fidgeted.

"I've never been good at these sorts of parties," Dane announced then looked around. "I'm not sure I fit in."

"That's because you're not properly accessorized." Collin linked Candy onto Dane's arm and grinned proudly. "There. Much better. This is Candy," he cheerfully introduced the woman, "as in arm--"

"You're the guy with the diamonds, right?" Candy announced in a giddy tone.

Dane eyed the voluptuous woman in the revealing dress and fidgeted. "Uh, I suppose."

"I love diamonds," she announced and giggled while clinging to him.

Collin grinned slyly and patted Dane on the shoulder. "Go on--make friends," he announced cheerfully. "I'm sure the two of you will have plenty to talk about."

"Collin, I'm not very comfortable--"

"Have a few more drinks," Collin insisted then handed Dane a small bag containing a white, powdery substance. "This will help you relax."

Dane looked at what was almost certainly cocaine in the small bag and immediately shook his head while attempting to return it. "No, Collin, I don't want that and neither should you."

Candy took it from Dane while warmly squeezing his hand. "I'll hold onto it for you," she announced and stuffed it down the front of her dress.

Dane was about to protest to his friend when Collin led Jasmine away. Dane looked at Candy, who smiled while clinging affectionately to him.

"Collin says you found some rare diamond and that you're worth a small fortune now," Candy cooed.

"Wasn't that nice of him to mention that," Dane muttered with some irritation.

"I thought so," Candy replied then grinned. "Want to go back to your place for some fun? We have everything we need for an amazing night." Candy playfully dipped her finger down her cleavage while smiling lustfully at him.

Dane stared at her, taken by surprise, while following her finger with his eyes. An image flashed of him with a woman rolling beneath the sheets on an antique bed. The unprovoked image was enough to startle him. Dane uncertainly looked away from Candy, tensed, and stared at his glass of brandy as if attempting to recapture the image he'd just seen.

"Did you hear me?" she announced while tilting her head. "That was an offer for wild sex."

Dane twitched as if he didn't even hear the comment. A rush of images exploded in his mind, but they came and went too fast to capture them. There was another image of Dane and the same woman making love. She pinned him to the bed. Dane was finally able to see the woman's face. Harley stared at him while grinning. Dane suddenly dropped his glass. It shattered, alerting everyone within the penthouse. Candy eyed the broken glass by their feet then smiled at Dane.

"Yeah, I get that reaction a lot," Candy giggled. "Ready to go?"

Dane pulled away from her and hurried through the balcony doors. He rushed across the balcony, approached the railing, and clung to it a moment while breathing rapidly. He stared across the dark city while almost gasping and attempted to relax. He then heard a woman's scream. Dane looked down with alarm. He saw the same woman from his vision clinging to the last rung of the balcony railing. Dane gasped and lunged for her hand. He held onto her wrist to keep her from falling.

"Help Murdock!" the attractive woman screamed.

Dane stared helplessly at the young woman and attempted to pull her up. She was suddenly gone. He uncertainly looked around with a startled gasp then held his head a moment as he sank into thought.

"What's going on?" he gasped softly. "Did someone drug my drink?" His eyes suddenly narrowed as anger set in. "Collin, you bastard."

He looked beyond the city to the distant harbor. A beacon shined from across the harbor. It appeared to be coming from some sort of lighthouse outside the city. The lights on the buildings appeared to fade before his eyes, leaving only the lighthouse. He watched the approaching storm as lightning flashed across the distant ocean. The light from the lighthouse beacon shined into the ocean reflecting off an old yacht as it sailed through the rough waters. Dane stared into the dark night with a look of surprise and possible horror.

"A vintage yacht?" He clutched the railing and stared at the balcony while deep in thought. "Vintage yacht," he again whispered. "Lighthouse?" He then considered the comment. "She's waiting in the lighthouse." Dane looked beyond the city and past the harbor to the lighthouse that he could barely see. "She's watching for the vintage yacht from the lighthouse. Who's this woman? I know her. She's a--a housekeeper--an innkeeper?" His eyes suddenly widened.

158

"She's a witch!" Dane stared off while deep in thought. "Where is she? Where's the witch?"

The thunder rumbled in the near distance. The dark clouds rolled across the sky. Lightning in the distance lit up what appeared to be a large resort with a lighthouse near the cliffs. Dane stared at the faraway lighthouse in silence while remaining deep in thought.

Chapter Thirty-six

*H*arley stood behind the check-in desk while working on the computer. As she stared at the screen, she groaned softly with defeat and allowed her head to fall onto the counter.

"One good summer. Is that really asking too much?" she muttered softly then resumed typing on the computer with disgust while shaking her head. "I'm never going to get that business improvement loan with only 50% occupancy this summer."

She heard the thunder in the distance growing louder. Harley looked toward the lobby windows as lightning flashed and brightened the outside world. She rolled her eyes and groaned at the prospect of more water damage from another heavy storm.

"I'm sure I'll find a new leak by morning," she muttered with disgust. The power went out leaving her in near darkness. "Right on cue."

She looked around the dark lobby and waited a moment. Nothing happened.

"And of course the backup generator doesn't automatically come on like it's supposed to," she snapped. "I wish just one thing worked as it's supposed to around here."

Harley snatched a flashlight from beneath the front desk and headed for the long corridor past the elevators.

"I just love that basement in the dark," she muttered. "Creepy, spider infested junkyard."

✝

*H*arley walked through the dark basement by the gleam of her flashlight. The light lent an eerie glow to the strange objects stored within the basement. The image of a man, unbeknownst to her, was present in the shadows as she passed. Harley paused before the large generator, took a moment to glance over the monstrosity, and then pressed a button. Nothing happened. Harley stared at the generator a moment with disbelief. She pressed the button again but still nothing. She pressed the button several more times and cried out with anger.

"Piece of crap!"

She heard a clatter across the basement, causing her to turn quickly. She shined her flashlight across the room, scanning the area. The flashlight created shadows on every wall from the clutter of stored objects. Something moved across the basement, or at least she thought she saw something move. Harley attempted to follow the moving object with her flashlight, but she couldn't locate it. Something then touched her shoulder. She turned with a startled scream and shined the light behind her. There was no one there. Soft voices were heard whispering around her. She again looked around with a startled gasp.

The voices whispered, "en forskyvning I tid; noen er tapt."

Harley looked around, uncertain of what she'd heard. "Is someone there?"

There was no response. A cold breeze blew past her. Harley again jumped and appeared alarmed. It wasn't the first time she'd encountered strange happenings within the basement or the hotel for that matter. She didn't want to believe in ghosts, but they seemed reluctant to abide by her wishes. Being alone in the darkness of the basement with a possible ghostly presence was almost more than she could handle. She hurried across the basement while shining her light all around her and headed for the stairs.

Once she reached the stairs, she practically ran up them. She hurried past the kitchen. The whispering voices were behind her, almost as if they were following her.

"en forskyvning I tid; noen er tapt."

What were they saying? She wasn't sure she wanted to know. They'd rarely spoken to her before, and she wished they'd return to their silent hauntings. The ghostly voices appeared to be gaining on her, frightening her.

"en forskyvning I tid; noen er tapt," the ghostly voices continued but now closer.

Harley looked behind her as she headed along the corridor for the lobby while attempting to outrun the ghostly voices. She entered the lobby and suddenly collided with someone. Harley screamed in response and whipped her head in the direction of the person before her, shinning her light on him. Rhodes held onto her shoulders to keep her from falling and grinned while chuckling at her mild hysteria. She was glad someone was amused by her fear.

"What's the matter, Harley?" Rhodes teased. "Afraid of the dark?"

Harley took a step back to put some distance between them and attempted to act casual despite her anxieties.

"No, just very big spiders," she informed him while fidgeting. "If you'll excuse me, I need to find Murdock to start the backup generator."

She briskly walked past him. The last thing she wanted was to be alone with Rhodes in the dark. Rhodes turned and followed her. She watched him out of the corner of her eye as he kept pace with her. She didn't know why he frightened her the way he did. He was probably harmless, but she always felt as if he were stalking her, attempting to corner her.

"I can help with the generator," he insisted.

Being alone with Rhodes, in the dark, in the creepy basement was the last thing she wanted or needed. Without looking back at the man following her, she responded, "Thanks, but my insurance company wouldn't approve."

As she continued into the lobby, Harley glanced behind her. Rhodes continued along the corridor in the opposite direction toward the stairs. She was grateful he lost interest and went his own way. A light suddenly shined in her face, startling her. Harley jumped with surprise and stared at the light, momentarily frozen from it. The flashlight lowered to reveal Murdock with a mocking grin on his face.

"You're certainly jumpy," he teased at her expense. "See another ghost?"

"Worse," Harley muttered while attempting to relax and rubbed her chilled arms while darting looks around the dark room. "I ran into Rhodes in the dark."

Murdock's frown resembled a sneer. "You're right, that is worse," he muttered. "Problem with the generator again, or were you too afraid to go down there by yourself?"

"As usual, I couldn't start it."

He shook his head with disgust. "You need to call that salesman back out and have that piece of crap replaced," Murdock informed her in a firm tone.

"It's on my 'to do' list right after buying groceries," she muttered.

"Come on," he announced with a sigh. "Let's have a look at that oversized paperweight."

Harley stared across the lobby with a strange look of silent horror. She grabbed Murdock's hand and stopped him. He looked across the dimly lit lobby in the direction she stared. Harley slowly approached the pool of fresh blood on the stone in the middle of the lobby floor. Murdock eyed her suspiciously.

"What is it?" Murdock asked.

"It's blood," she gasped softly then looked at him with alarm. "Don't you see it?"

Murdock groaned softly and turned her away from where she stared and forced her toward the main corridor. "No more ghosts tonight, Harley," he announced firmly. "You can wig out tomorrow all you want."

Harley was about to protest when the front door flew open from the heavy wind and rain. Both hurried across the lobby to shut the door and nearly collided with a soaking wet Remy, who had just entered. Harley and Remy screamed with surprise. Their startled screams alarmed Murdock, causing him to clutch his chest while groaning.

"What's with you two?" Murdock cried out.

"Something has me unsettled tonight," Harley announced while feeling tense.

"Me too," Remy gasped softly and rubbed her wet arms while looking around.

Murdock studied Remy a moment then appeared curious. "I thought you were working at the tavern," he remarked.

"The place was dead," Remy replied. "They sent me home early."

"I'm surprised you didn't stay at the tavern to avoid our guests from hell," Murdock muttered.

"I considered it," Remy gently informed him, "but I felt I should come back early."

"Let's get that generator working before the guests start complaining," Murdock announced.

Murdock turned to head toward the basement. Remy caught his arm, stopping him. He looked at the concerned look on her face with some surprise.

"What?" he asked.

"Something's wrong," Remy announced and again looked around. "I have this feeling--"

"Yeah, me too," Harley replied as her eyes widened to her friend's comment. "Like deja vu."

"I think you're both insane," Murdock scoffed. "Nothing a few drinks won't cure. I'll get the generator running; you fix some martinis in the office."

As Murdock turned, both women grabbed either arm startling him.

"No--" Remy cried out.

"We should stick together," Harley added.

"What's with you two?"

"I have this terrible feeling something bad is about to happen," Remy informed him. "Make fun of me all you want later but humor me just this once."

Murdock stared at the strange look on both women's faces. It was obvious he was slightly rattled by their expressions. "Okay, fine," he muttered softly under his breath, although they obviously had gotten to him. "We'll go to the basement together." He shook his head. "Women!"

Chapter Thirty-seven

Murdock fiddled with the generator within the cluttered basement. Remy and Harley stood close to each other and glanced around with shared looks of dread. After pressing the same button Harley had, the generator started with a loud grinding sound. The emergency lights came on, providing only dim lighting. Murdock turned away from the generator, pleased with himself, and then frowned when he noticed his friends' expressions.

"You two are really spooked tonight," he announced with astonishment then shook his head. "We're not all going to fit in my bed, you know."

"In your dreams, Murdock," Remy scoffed while attempting a tough appearance as she folded her arms across her chest. Her tough girl act was short lived, indicated by her trembling body.

"Don't be too hasty, Remy," Harley muttered while looking around as she clutched her own shoulders. "I don't like this feeling I'm having." She subconsciously shivered. "Almost as if death is stalking me."

"Not exactly the same feeling I'm having," Remy informed her timidly. "I'm having this overwhelming feeling of loss. Like someone close to me just died."

Murdock stared at both women then subconsciously shivered from their comments. He immediately brushed it off and took a tough stance.

"Okay, that's enough from both of you," he suddenly proclaimed. "No one is dying and death is not stalking either of you. My God, PMS must be hell!"

His assurances didn't change the way Harley felt. Despite her mood, she drew a deep breath and nervously looked around. "We should probably check on our guests," Harley announced gently. "Make sure they're okay. Maybe take them flashlights. We're only operating on 20% power with that thing running. The guests won't be happy about that."

"I think we should lock ourselves in one of our rooms and wait until the power comes back on," Remy remarked in all seriousness.

"You can do that, but I have a responsibility to my guests," Harley informed her.

"Why don't the two of lock yourselves in one of your bedrooms. Please, by all means, have a few drinks and calm down," Murdock announced sternly. "I'll check on our guests." He eyed them and raised his brows. "Would that make the two of you happy?"

Remy and Harley exchanged looks and appeared unconvinced that his suggestion would do any good.

"Do you have your master key?" Harley nervously asked. "You could take mine."

"No, that's okay," Murdock replied. "I'll grab mine from behind the front desk on my way through."

†

*A*fter leaving his friends safely in the staff wing, Murdock walked along the corridor toward the elevators. He paused before the elevator door and pressed the button. As he waited for the elevator, a cool breeze blew past him, causing him to shiver. He looked around then felt a feeling of dread sweeping over him. The elevator dinged, startling him. He jumped as the doors opened then attempted to relax and groaned softly.

"Now they've got me doing it," he muttered while shaking his head as he entered the elevator.

He pressed the button and caught of glimpse of his reflection in the metal control panel. Blood ran down his neck and soaked into his shirt. Murdock did a double take while subconsciously reaching for his neck and looked back into the reflective metal of the control panel. His neck was dry and there was no blood. He uncertainly looked at his hand then drew a shaken breath.

"What the hell--?"

He again stared at his reflection in the control panel then sank into thought. Murdock looked at his arm and witnessed the tiny hairs standing on end. His hand began to tremble. A bewildered look crossed his face. He controlled his trembling hand and reached for the third floor button. Blood seeped from the button and ran down the control panel. Murdock cried out and slammed his finger repeatedly against the 'open' button. The elevator stopped and the doors slid open. Murdock bolted from the elevator and nearly fell to the corridor floor.

Chapter Thirty-eight

*H*arley paced before the bay window within her living quarters while Remy, who had now changed into dry clothing, sat on the sofa and clutched a pillow to her chest. Harley stared at the barely visible lighthouse at the opposite end of the hotel. It seemed creepy with the beacon out. She wished she could have convinced Murdock to start the lighthouse generator, but he'd never go out there in the pouring rain for something so frivolous. Both women remained unusually distracted and in their own paranoid worlds. Neither had spoken in nearly twenty minutes, leaving the room deathly silent except for the loud rumbling of thunder and the second hand clicking on the table clock. The relentlessly ticking clock suddenly stopped, leaving them in silence. Both looked at the clock. A loud crack of thunder caused both women to jump and look at the storm beyond the window. As they collected themselves from their overreaction, Harley turned to face Remy with a pale look on her face.

"I'm worried about Murdock," Harley remarked while vigorously raking her fingers through her hair, subconsciously scratching her scalp with her fingernails. "I don't understand why I'm so worried."

Remy looked up at her friend and clutched the pillow so hard she nearly tore it. "Yeah, I'm worried too."

"Should we go after him?"

"Maybe we should," Remy remarked and unfolded her legs from beneath her. She then hesitated and fidgeted nervously. "I don't suppose your father owned a gun."

"No, I don't think so," Harley replied then gave the comment some consideration. "Although the cook kept a baseball bat in the kitchen pantry."

"We can grab that on our way through and take the backstairs to the guestrooms," Remy informed her.

"That's a good plan," Harley replied. "We should run into Murdock on the third floor."

"Do you have an extra flashlight?" Remy asked. "The kitchen will only be dimly lit with the emergency lights."

"Yeah, in my bedroom," Harley announced then hurried into her nearby bedroom.

Harley felt around the nightstand alongside her bed then opened the top drawer and easily found the unusually bright, compact flashlight. She turned on the flashlight and instinctively scanned her room with it. The flashlight passed a large mass beneath her covers. Harley quickly returned the light to the object under her covers and stared at the bloodied sheet.

"Remy," she cried out in fear then held her breath and reached for the sheet.

Remy ran into the room as Harley pulled back the blood-soaked sheet. Harley cried out at the sight of the mutilated caretaker's wife from decades past lying on the bed, drenched in her own blood. She had been repeatedly hacked with an ax and was almost beyond recognition. Harley screamed causing Remy to cry out as well.

"What is it?" Remy screamed in horror. "Is it a spider?"

Harley nearly choked and looked back at her friend. She couldn't believe Remy's response. "You don't see it?" she almost demanded.

"See what?" Remy cried out while looking around the empty bed with wide, terror-filled eyes.

Harley looked back at the bed and stared at the excessively clean, white sheets. The dead woman was gone! It had been another ghostly manifestation that only she could see. Harley caught her breath then groaned softly while walking past her friend.

"Never mind," she muttered.

Remy again looked around the room while shivering, possibly looking for signs of a spider. She then turned and hurried after her friend.

†

𝓜urdock walked along the third floor hallway while subconsciously running his fingers repeatedly through his hair. The incident in the elevator had rattled him more than he was willing to admit. He paused before the first occupied room, collected himself, and firmly knocked on the door.

"Blaine," he announced through the door. "Rollcall, buddy. Just checking to make sure everyone is okay."

There was no response. He knocked again, this time a little louder. Blaine still didn't respond. Murdock frowned and was about to walk away when he heard a clunk from within the room. He hesitated and removed his master key.

"Blaine, I'm coming in."

Murdock unlocked the door with the master key and slowly opened it to reveal the mostly dark, silent room. He uncertainly entered and paused just within the doorway. Murdock flipped the light switch, allowing the emergency light to come on. Blaine lie on the floor on the opposite side of the bed near an overturned nightstand. Murdock gasped with alarm, hurried toward him, and crouched alongside him.

"Blaine, are you okay?"

Murdock turned him over then immediately tensed. Blood saturated the man's shirt. The tears in his shirt revealed he'd been brutally stabbed several times. Blaine managed to look at him, gasped a shallow breath, and then fell limp. Murdock released him with a startled gasp, allowing him to fall onto his back. Murdock sprang to his feet, hesitated only a moment, and then ran from the room. He ran into the hallway while removing his cell phone from his pocket. The only place he'd possibly get reception was the roof. He needed to get the police but driving to town and leaving his friends behind was not an option. Murdock ran down the hall toward the fire stairs. He heard a woman's shrill scream from one of the nearby rooms. Murdock hesitated, stared at the vacant room with the door propped open, and uncertainly entered. He stopped just inside the room to see an unfamiliar man with a gun standing over a naked man and woman cowering on the king-sized bed while holding the sheets to their bodies.

Murdock was about to yell when the man standing over the bed fired several shots into the naked couple scrambling to jump out from under the covers. He watched the naked man and woman take several shots each but was unable to do more than stand there. It only took him a second to figure out they were ghosts, and it wasn't real. Murdock watched with wide eyes as the man placed the barrel of the gun in his mouth and squeezed the trigger. Flesh and blood exploded out the back of his head and spattered against the wall. Murdock stared in horror as the man collapsed onto the bed with the naked couple. He'd never believed Harley's stories about ghosts within the hotel, but he was suddenly proved wrong. He was left with only one course of action. Murdock cried out and ran from the room. As he ran into the hallway screaming like a madman, Bernie and Kaplan appeared from their room and watched him run down the hallway. They exchanged looks, shrugged, and returned to their room.

✝

$\mathcal{M}$urdock ran from the elevator stopped within the lobby and headed for the front desk. He was about to go behind the desk when he heard a gunshot. He looked across the lobby and saw the ghostly sailor, Edward, take a bullet to the chest. Walter's ghost charged Albert and attempted to take the gun away from him. The ghostly apparitions struggled for control of the gun. A shot was fired, but both men continued to fight for the gun. There was another shot. Walter finally collapsed to the floor. Albert panted heavily while staring at his fallen friend now dead on the floor, his blood rapidly spilling into a pool beneath him. Albert then looked at his own shirt as blood seeped through it. He touched the wound and stared at the blood on his fingers with a stunned look. He attempted to seek help but stumbled and collapsed to the floor. Murdock watched the haunting scene unfold while panting as his heart raced. He then saw a woman in a white nightgown outside on the terrace beyond the glass windows. He was almost certain it was Harley and his expression shattered.

"Harley?" he suddenly gasped then bolted for the terrace doors.

Murdock ran into the pouring rain and looked around the terrace. He saw the woman slip through the opening between the overgrown hedges.

"Harley!"

He ran in the pouring rain after the woman, who was now out of view. Murdock slipped through the overgrown hedges then suddenly stopped in the clearing on the other side. He saw the woman dressed only in a nightgown climb over the split rail fencing to the cliff side. Murdock's look was terrified.

"Harley! No!"

Murdock ran for the woman. When he saw her profile, he realized it wasn't Harley and skidded to a stop in the wet grass. The woman leaped from the cliff to the jagged rocks below. Murdock stared with horror and held his drenched forehead.

"What the hell is going on around here?" he gasped then looked back at the hotel. Alarm swept over him. "Don't worry, girls. I'm coming!"

Murdock ran toward the overgrown hedges then suddenly stopped to see the caretaker dragging his bloodied ax alongside him as he headed toward the workshop. Murdock stopped, unable to move, and watched the ghostly man from decades past covered in blood. The caretaker approached the old wood chipper and flicked a switch. The wood chipper churned with an eerie sound. Murdock watched only a second longer as the caretaker crawled inside the chipper hopper. The horror showed on Murdock's face.

"No!"

The man was sucked into the chipper as he cried out in genuine agony. Ground up, bloodied human flesh shot out the other end, painting the entire yard with a large swath of blood. His bones could be heard grinding within the churning blades. Murdock cringed and looked away.

Chapter Thirty-nine

Remy and Harley entered the dimly lit kitchen with some caution as both remained tense and mostly out of sorts. The massive kitchen was filled with shadows cast upon the walls, which wasn't helping ease their unfounded tensions any. It seemed odd that the kitchen was darker than usual, even with the generator running. Harley then realized it was because the lighthouse beacon was no longer illuminated, which typically gave a slight glow to the kitchen even when it was completely dark. Both women put their concerns aside when a strange odor within the kitchen assaulted their senses. They uncertainly looked around then at each another.

"Do you smell something?" Harley asked.

"Smells like smoke," Remy remarked.

Both looked around the nearly dark kitchen. There was a strange glow coming from the back just near the stoves. Remy's eyes widened with horror as she pointed.

"Fire!"

Remy sprang into action, grabbing a nearby fire extinguisher, and ran across the kitchen toward the fire that hadn't yet been big enough to activate the fire sprinklers. Harley bolted to the nearby pull station and, without hesitation, pulled the fire alarm. Lights flashed and the alarm wailed, alerting the entire hotel of the situation. Once the fire alarm had been activated, Harley then ran for a second fire extinguisher just across the kitchen so she could join Remy in fighting the fire. Halfway to the second fire extinguisher, Harley suddenly skidded to a stop as the caretaker's ax thrust downward at her. She screamed and crouched down as the ax passed through her and into the screaming cook behind her. Harley bolted out of the way and turned in time to see the caretaker repeatedly hacking the fallen cook with his bloodied ax. Harley turned with alarm and nearly collided with someone within the dim lighting. Rhodes caught her shoulders and appeared concerned while staring into her terrified eyes.

"Are you okay?" he gasped with surprise then looked around. "Is that the fire alarm?"

Harley stared at him a moment and felt paralyzed with fear. Images of Rhodes and Murdock struggling for a bloody knife flashed through her mind. She stared at the blood covering Rhodes' shirt and hands and pulled away while glaring at him with horror.

"It was you!"

Rhodes was stunned by her sudden outburst and the look on her face. "What are you talking about?" he demanded.

"You killed him," she cried out and indicated his shirt. "You're covered in his blood!"

Rhodes continued to stare at her with astonishment then looked at his clean, white shirt with confusion. Harley looked back at his shirt and realized there was no blood on it. She wondered what the hell she had just seen. Remy hurried toward them with her fire extinguisher while breathing heavily.

"Disaster diverted," Remy announced with relief then eyed the eerie exchange between her friend and Rhodes. She immediately fidgeted. "Did I interrupt something?"

"Your boss just accused me of killing one of my friends," he announced then indicated his clean shirt, "because I'm covered in blood."

Remy looked at Rhodes for any traces of blood then glanced at Harley with bewilderment. "There's no blood, Harley." She easily brushed off the accusation and took Harley's arm without hesitation. "Come on, the fire department will be here any minute. We need to get everyone to the gazebo."

Harley stared at Rhodes and remained horrified. "I never said you killed one of your friends." Her eyes widened. "It was Blaine," she gasped with an odd realization. "You killed Blaine!"

Remy gripped the fire extinguisher and was about to raise it defensively when Rhodes suddenly punched her in the face. She was thrown across the kitchen and to the floor, the fire extinguisher clattering against the tile as it fell from her grip. Before Harley could even cry out, Rhodes attempted to grab her. She let out a shrill scream and jumped away from him with horror clearly in her eyes. From a hidden holster behind his back, Rhodes removed a large hunting knife stained with blood. As he stared at her, his look was demented but almost humored.

"I don't know how you figured it out, but you're not going to talk."

Harley cried out, bolted away from him, and ran for the backstairs. She threw the door open and thundered up the steps. As Harley ran up the stairs, Rhodes chased after her. He was closing in fast, his longer legs scaling the steps two at a time. Harley made it to the second floor and attempted to open the stairwell door. Rhodes was directly behind her and thrust downward with the knife. She bolted away from the door, narrowly missing the bloodstained blade. It hit the metal door with a metallic clang and a slight spark. Harley kicked him in the knee, only buying herself precious seconds. She bolted up the second flight of stairs for the third floor and threw open the door. She ran into the third floor corridor while fumbling to remove her master key from her pocket. She stopped at the first room on the right, unlocked the door, and bolted inside.

Harley attempted to shut the door behind her, but Rhodes plowed into it, sending her flying across the room and onto the bed. She rolled across the bed with the bounce, jumped off facing Rhodes, and darted looks around the room for an exit. Rhodes charged for her with the bloody knife clutched in his hand. She had nowhere to go! As he plunged downward with the knife, Harley caught his wrist and was nearly driven to her knees by the force. She planted her foot into his abdomen and threw herself backwards. Rhodes was thrown over her and into the glass, balcony doors. The glass doors shattered as Rhodes struck them. Harley barely looked back as she ran for the closed guestroom door.

"Harley!" Remy was heard screaming from the hallway just outside the locked door.

Harley ran for the door and turned the knob, but Rhodes was already on his feet and charging for her. He thrust the knife downward. Harley screamed and bolted away from the now partially open door. Her master key fell to the floor just outside the slightly ajar door. Rhodes stopped his downward thrust midway, spun toward Harley with an evil look on his face, and leaped for her. Harley bolted from his path, but he caught her around the neck. Rhodes slung her out the broken balcony doors with such force that she flew across the balcony and catapulted over the railing. Harley caught the rail on the other side and screamed as she dangled. Rhodes stepped onto the balcony before her, stared at her only a moment, and prepared to slash the helpless woman.

Remy suddenly jumped onto Rhodes back and caught his wrist, stopping his attack. Rhodes struggled against Remy, who held him from behind while riding his back. Her arms and legs were locked around him resembling a human backpack. She was wiry; she was athletic; and she determined not to let go. Every imaginable curse word spew from Remy's mouth. She was no longer afraid; she was a demon possessed. Harley looked beyond her feet where she dangled. There was a small area of concrete three stories below before the jagged cliffs leading to the ocean beneath. Either landing would kill her. Harley gasped and attempted to pull herself up enough to get her feet to the balcony ledge. Her foot slipped twice on the wet ledge.

Harley looked into the hotel room through the broken glass doors. Remy continued to ride Rhodes' back while clinging to his wrist as he attempted to toss her from him. She had to help her friend! Harley almost had her footing. She suddenly lost her grip on the wet railing and nearly plummeted. She caught the vertical rung as her legs now dangled below the balcony. She again looked through the broken balcony doors. Rhodes managed to toss Remy off his back and immediately leaped on top of her where she was now crouched. He clutched her throat and was about to plunge the knife into her neck. Harley could only stare helplessly at her friend who was about to die before her eyes.

"No!" she cried out with horror.

Remy kicked Rhodes in the knee, sending them both to the floor alongside the bed and just out of Harley's sight. Fearing for her friend's life, Harley made a bold move to pull herself up and lost her grip. A hand suddenly caught her wrist, stopping her from falling and causing her to scream with surprise. Harley looked up to see the familiar face of a man she was certain she'd never met. Dane half hung over the railing while clinging to her wrist. Harley's mind was reeling at the sight of the man as images of their last meeting flashed through her subconscious. She pushed all thoughts aside while catching the rail with her free hand. None of that mattered at the moment.

"Help Remy!"

Dane stared at Harley in possible disbelief while clinging to her wrist. Their eyes locked for only a second. It was almost as if they'd done this before yet it somehow seemed different. As if on command, Dane released her wrist and ran back into the guestroom. Remy leaped to her feet and attempted to escape Rhodes. He slammed her into the dresser and prepared to plunge the knife into her throat. Dane charged for Rhodes as he thrust downward with the knife and tackled him to the floor. Remy was thrown across the room from the force of Dane tackling Rhodes. Dane and Rhodes rolled together several times across the worn carpet. Rhodes landed on top of Dane, coiled back with the knife, and attempted to stab him in the throat. Dane caught his wrist with both hands and held the knife back.

Remy weakly stumbled onto the balcony and attempted to pull Harley to safety. Harley managed to get her foot onto the balcony and pull herself up while Remy pulled on her pants belt. As Harley stood on the balcony on the opposite side of the railing, she saw Remy staring past her toward the ocean with her mouth hanging open and a shocked look on her face. Harley briefly looked behind her as she climbed over the railing to the safety of the balcony. She suddenly understood Remy's expression.

The vintage yacht sailed on the rough waters in the distance, but there was no lighthouse beacon to guide it. Harley stared only a moment before returning to reality. She bolted past Remy and into the guestroom. Harley ran for Rhodes, who was now on top of Dane, and kicked him in the face. He was violently thrown off Dane. Dane scrambled to his feet as Rhodes leaped up with the knife still in his hand and charged for him. Dane ran for Rhodes and rammed his shoulder into Rhodes' chest, driving him onto the balcony. The powerful hit sent Rhodes flying backwards, toppling him over the balcony railing. He dropped the knife and caught the upper railing with one hand. Rhodes clung to the railing while dangling from the balcony and frantically attempted to pull himself up to safety.

"Need a hand?" Remy snarled from above him.

Rhodes looked up to see Remy standing over him on the balcony side with a twisted smirk on her face. She punched him in the face. Rhodes lost his grip on the railing and plummeted from the balcony. Remy looked over the railing with a scowl on her face while gingerly shaking her sore hand. Rhodes lie broken and bloody on the stone terrace floor just beyond the hot tub, narrowly missing the cliff. Remy smirked with satisfaction. Harley and Dane appeared on the balcony and looked down as well. Their attention immediately shifted to the ocean. The vintage yacht was now dangerously close to the reef and fought the harsh waves. Remy and Harley stared with surprise and then horror.

"It's them! It's my parents!"

"We have to get the lighthouse beacon working or they'll crash on the rocks," Remy cried out.

"There's no time!"

"What do we do?" Remy gasped while staring helplessly at her friend.

Harley stared back with an unpredictable look in her eyes. Her serious look was alarming to her friend.

"We need to set the room on fire," Harley announced while springing into action.

"Are you insane?" Remy cried out and caught her friend before she could gather flammable material.

"We need to do something," Harley gasped. "We only have seconds to save them!"

Dane looked from the yacht barely staying on top of the crashing waves then to his hands. He took a deep breath, placed his hands together, and then exhaled while pulling them apart. A blue ball of glowing light remained within his hands. Harley and Remy stared at the small ball of light he held, shock clearly on their faces. Harley then met his gaze.

"It's not big enough," she managed to gasp softly. "They'll never see it."

Dane took a step back, coiled back his arm in his best pitcher's form, and threw the ball of light for the nearby lighthouse. The blue light shattered the glass with a thunderous crash then engulfed the lighthouse lantern room, shining brilliantly across the ocean and the entire area surrounding the hotel. Despite the surprise on the faces of Harley and Remy, neither were nearly as surprised as Dane had been. They looked back at the ocean, now bright as day, and saw the yacht avoid the large rocks as it turned toward the brightly lit beach and dock. Both women uncertainly looked back at Dane.

"I'm not even going to ask," Remy announced firmly while holding her hand up to him and casually walked past him into the guestroom.

Harley stared at Dane a moment longer then shook her head with disbelief. "I have a lot of questions right now," she announced. "But they'll have to wait until later."

Harley hurried into the guestroom after Remy. Dane looked from his empty hands to the blue, glowing light shining within the lighthouse. He shook his head with disbelief.

"I have a few questions of my own," he muttered to himself then hurried after the women.

Chapter Forty

$\mathcal{T}$he elevator dinged just before the doors opened to the lobby. Harley, Dane, and Remy hurried from the elevator as Murdock entered the lobby through the front door. Fire truck sirens wailed outside the hotel, indicating the fire department was already on the scene. Murdock saw his friends, hurried toward them, and hugged both women.

"I was worried about you," he announced while pulling back and appeared frightened then oddly angry. "Blaine's been murdered." He could barely control his emotions. "When I went to the staff wing to find you, I heard the fire alarm sounding. Neither of you were there. What happened?"

"It's a long story," Harley muttered.

Murdock eyed Dane suspiciously and cocked his head. "Who are you? Where the hell did you come from?"

"I drove in from the city," Dane casually replied, "but that's a long story too."

Murdock remained baffled while staring at Dane. "You look familiar. Have we met?"

"That's an even longer story," Dane reluctantly informed him with a sigh.

"We have a boat to catch," Harley announced and bolted past her friend.

"What?" Murdock asked while spinning to watch her run across the lobby for the terrace door.

Harley ran for the door and nearly collided with Bernie, Kaplan, Patrice, and Decker as they entered. They attempted to stop her and began complaining in unison. Harley ignored their ranting and ran past them onto the terrace. Murdock, Remy, and Dane hurried after her.

†

*T*he vintage yacht was already tied off at the private dock on the secluded beach beneath the hotel as Harley ran across the sand. Harley's parents, Rollin and Rita, hurried along the dock as Harley ran for them. It was a tearful reunion as they hugged her with relief. All three sobbed with joy as the rain soaked them.

"I can't believe you're here," Harley sobbed while smiling. "I wanted to believe you were still alive, but--" She wiped her tears away despite the rain soaking her body. "It's been over a year. How?"

Murdock, Remy, and Dane hurried onto the dock to join them. Rollin and Rita exchanged looks, eyed Harley with surprise to her comment, and appeared stunned.

"Over a year?" Rollin nearly laughed. "Are you feeling okay? We just left this morning."

"Okay, now I'm really confused," Murdock announced as the rain soaked him where he stood alongside the equally soaked Remy. "Someone needs to explain what's going on here."

"Maybe Harley's parents can explain," Dane replied, catching everyone's attention.

Rollin and Rita appeared bewildered as they stared at the unfamiliar man in the drenched, expensive suit.

"Do we know you?" Rita asked while tilting her head slightly to the side.

181

"Honestly, I don't think I know anyone here," Dane informed her casually, "but if I'm not mistaken, I think the answer is in your wine cellar."

Rita and Rollin stared at Dane with surprise as their mouths fell open. They exchanged looks and fidgeted from the comment. It was obvious they understood the meaning.

"Oh--" Rita muttered.

"Yeah--oh," Rollin reluctantly added.

†

*E*veryone had changed into dry clothing and sat before a fire in the massive lobby fireplace. The police continued their investigation into Blaine's murder and Rhodes' body on the terrace between the cliff and the hot tub. The fire department had finished their assessment of the small kitchen fire and had already given them the 'all clear'. The remaining hotel guests had turned in for night, being it was already closing in on early morning. Murdock passed glasses of brandy to Harley's parents and his friends then joined them, sitting alongside Remy on the sofa. Dane sat on the coffee table with his drink in his hand. He eyed the heavy, tree trunk table beneath him, appeared curious, and subconsciously ran his free hand along the glazed bark edge. When Rollin continued with his story of their day trip, Dane gave him his full attention.

"A massive storm hit us while we were returning home," Rollin announced and shook his head with disbelief. "It was bad. I was struggling to keep *The Dream Catcher* afloat."

"I remember this huge wave," Rita added and drifted off a moment. She looked back at the others. "That must be when *it* happened."

"You put a spell on you and your husband, didn't you?" Dane asked.

"I assume I did," Rita reluctantly replied. "I had no idea it'd affect memory. It's not as if Rollin and I routinely cast spells on a daily basis. We sort of dabble and mostly just with the small stuff for fun."

"So we've been floating around the ocean reliving the same day over and over for more than a year?" Rollin asked while shaking his head, still unable to comprehend what was happening.

"I'm going to answer yes to that," Dane replied with a sigh. "Harley had a similar encounter when she and Murdock were attacked."

"I'm pretty sure I was the one attacked," Remy firmly corrected.

Dane cast a look at Remy and raised his brows. "You were; in take two," he replied then looked back at Rollin. "It all sort of came to me almost like a dream, but I'm sure it was reality in another dimension." He hesitated then continued. "When Harley learned she'd caused her own dimensional dilemma, we used your spell book to break the spell. What we didn't know is it would break the spell the two of you were under as well." He shifted in his seat and inhaled deeply. "Mind you, I'm only giving this my best guess from research I'd done on the subject. I, uh, have an interesting and complex family ancestry."

"And somehow all of this has something to do with the guy the coroner scraped off the terrace?" Rita questioned while indicating the terrace door.

"Yeah, and for the record, I quit," Remy firmly informed them.

Rita stared at Harley's young friend and gently tilted her head in question. "Did you work for us?"

"You two have a lot to catch up on," Remy replied with a sigh.

"Yeah, like a year's worth of catching up," Murdock informed them while smirking.

"I'm sure the rest can wait until morning," Rollin announced and affectionately took his wife's hand in his. "It's been one hell of a night. I'm exhausted."

Rollin and Rita stood, kissed Harley goodnight, and left the lobby. Harley stared after them and suddenly grimaced. Their room wasn't their room anymore, but she didn't have the heart to call after them. They'd find out soon enough.

"Oh, they're not going to like what I did to their apartment," Harley muttered softly.

Murdock snorted a soft laugh. "You may want to give them a few days to recover before showing them the financial statements as well, Harley," he casually informed her.

"Yeah, that could put a damper on their welcome home party," Harley muttered then sighed, allowing a smile to cross her face. "It'll work out. I'm just glad they're alive. Everything else can be fixed."

Murdock stood with a weary groan and stretched. "Well, it's nearly three in the morning," he announced. "I think I'm going to get a few hours' sleep before dealing with the mess in the kitchen and guestrooms."

"You can walk me to my room," Remy announced while smiling timidly. "I'm still a little freaked with the power out and only the backup generator running."

Murdock playfully extended his hand to her. Remy smiled and accepted it. He pulled her to her feet and nearly into his arms. Both smiled timidly and looked away with embarrassment. Murdock glanced at Harley and offered a weary smile.

"Goodnight, Harley," he announced without releasing Remy's hand. "Don't stay up too late."

"I won't," she replied with a soft laugh. "I think I could sleep for a month."

Murdock guided Remy across the lobby and walked with her past the elevators toward the staff wing. Harley appeared tense now that she was finally alone with the familiar man she didn't know. As she searched for something to say to him, Dane stood and returned his attention to the old coffee table. She leaned forward in her plush chair and watched him.

"You seem to have a fondness for that coffee table," Harley remarked. "Did you know that was here when they built the hotel? It's over one hundred years old."

She grimaced slightly, realizing she sounded like a historic tour guide in a failed attempt to make small talk in an uncomfortable situation. Dane nodded without looking at her and continued his inspection of the coffee table.

"It's strange," he announced as he studied the tree trunk table. "There are all these memories I seem to have resembling some sort of weird dream regarding this hotel and our time together. They seem so real and yet not real at all." He ran his hand along the glazed bark edge of the coffee table. "There was one thing in particular I remember seeing just before the spell was reversed. I just wonder--"

Harley was about to comment when Dane pushed on a large knot on the edge. Something clicked within the coffee table. He slid the entire top back to reveal a large compartment. Harley sprang to her feet and stared at the small antique chest within the compartment. Dane eyed Harley. She met his gaze.

"Is that--?"

Dane nodded and grinned. "I think so."

He struggled with the old, rusted latch then pulled the lid open. Both stared at the chest half filled with century old gold coins. Harley and Dane eyed the gold then exchanged looks and laughed softly.

"I think your money problems have been resolved," Dane cheerfully informed her.

She laughed as Dane closed the chest and replaced the tabletop over it into its original position, keeping the chest securely hidden.

"You're very good at finding treasure, aren't you?" she teased.

Dane shrugged while grinning. "I have a knack for being at the right place at the right time."

Harley's smile slowly faded as she stared at the man standing before her. He noted her look and tensed slightly.

"So, uh, all those fuzzy memories I'm having actually happened in an alternate dimension?" she asked.

"Yes," Dane replied then offered a tiny smile, "but they'll fade quickly."

Harley fidgeted slightly, but she had to ask the question foremost on her mind at that moment. "I remember something intimate between us," Harley announced timidly then lifted her eyes and met his gaze. "Was that real?"

"At the time, but not anymore," he reassured her. "It'll fade. Technically, it never happened. That's in some other dimension in some alternate time." He offered a knowing smile. "You're still 'a good girl'."

"Oh," she muttered and shifted in her seat while feeling her cheeks become hot and red with embarrassment. "You knew about that too, huh?"

"We had several lengthy, intimate talks," he replied then appeared tense as well and shifted uncomfortably. "I won't get in your way of happiness, Harley. What happened never happened. I'll stay the night and leave in the morning." He hesitated while staring at her. "I do, however, recommend you tell Murdock how you really feel about him."

She stared at him with some surprise then shook her head. "I don't even know what I really feel right now," Harley replied gently. "It's a jumble of images from the past, present, and alternate dimensions."

"You'll figure it out eventually," he replied then softly added, "just as I'm sure I'll eventually get over you."

Harley stared at him with a bewildered look. He kissed her gently on the cheek and left the lobby. She watched him leave while sinking deep into thought.

Chapter Forty-one

*F*ive o'clock in the morning. Dane lie awake in bed while staring out the partially open curtains at the distant ocean. Despite the hour, it appeared as if he hadn't slept at all. He heard the guestroom door unlocking. He uncertainly sat up and looked at the door as it opened. Harley stood in the doorway and offered a tiny smile.

"Apparently that worked better when I was supposedly a ghost, huh?" she teased gently.

He offered a warm smile. "I can't say I minded."

Harley allowed the door to close behind her and uncertainly approached the bed while appearing tense. Dane smiled gently and moved over on the bed. It was an odd recollection of something that never happened that they both shared. He suddenly tensed and appeared embarrassed.

"Sorry," he announced gently. "Old habit."

"It's okay," she announced then sat on the edge of the bed and stared into his eyes despite her uneasiness. "I thought a lot about

187

what you'd said earlier," she gently informed him. "I know it's insane, but I don't want those memories to fade away. Even if it was some other dimension that will never happen, it was still real to me. I don't want it to not be real."

Dane stared at her a moment in silence. He drew a quick, shallow breath. "If you want me to stay, I will."

She stared back at him then exhaled softly. "I want you to stay."

There was an odd silence as he stared at her. A tiny smile crossed his face. "Okay."

Harley appeared relieved and hugged him. He returned the embrace and gently nuzzled her face with his. She pulled back to meet his gaze with less certainty.

"Can I lie with you a while?" she asked gently.

Dane snorted a soft laugh and hid his grin. "You do remember what happened the last time you just wanted to lie with me, don't you?"

"Vaguely," she replied then smiled with more confidence. "I wouldn't mind a refresher."

Dane's expression dropped slightly. When he realized what she was suggesting, he hid his smile and kissed her warmly. As she returned the warm, passionate kiss, he gently lowered her to the bed.

The End

Other books by Holly Copella!
Reviews left on Amazon are appreciated!

"The Battle for Andrea Marie"

A cruise ship attack turns six survivors into overnight celebrities after they take credit for the heroic act of a stowaway who died saving them.

The cruise is just what Jess needed--a bit of harmless fun far from her daily grind. But what begins as a relaxing vacation turns into a desperate fight for her life when terrorists take over the ship and start piling up bodies. Teaming up with a mysterious stowaway, Jess attempts to send out a distress call but knows they cannot wait for help to come. If she or the few remaining passengers have any hope for survival, Jess must act now. The papers dub it "The Battle for *Andrea Marie*," but to Jess it is the moment she fought side-by-side with her enigmatic Romeo, saving the ship--and losing him. She thinks the story ends there, but really, the nightmare is just beginning...

"Insanely Deadly"

When the dead return to life, it's up to an admiral's daughter and a mildly insane, former war hero to save their small town.

Jetta Cross, a Navy Admiral's daughter, is tasked with keeping her father's comrade, a former war hero turned town crazy, grounded in the real world. Capt. John Hunter is still fighting the war in his head, where imaginary dead people are part of his world. When a viral outbreak brings about a zombie uprising, Hunter is left to his own devices. He must resume his role as a one-man commando unit in order to destroy the ravenous undead. With Hunter still fighting his own inner demons as well as the undead, the townspeople fear their zombie neighbors may not be the only threat. Stranded at the island's luxurious resort with a handful of workers, Jetta is forced to live up to her father's reputation and take charge of the deteriorating situation at the hotel. She must wage her own war against the infected before the government declares her hometown a total loss.

"Deadly Institution"

A town recluse suspected of killing his wife teams up with a young woman in order to stop a killer.

After being accused of murdering his wife, Konrad Asher turns his back on the town that once adored him. Ten years later, he still holds his grudge and the title of the most feared man in town. With the reopening of the burned mental institution, where his wife had died, former employees are now murdered one-by-one, throwing suspicion back on Asher. A young local reporter, Jacey, is forced to reveal her long-time friendship with the infamous recluse in order to clear his name not only in the recent murders but to exonerate him in the death of his wife as well. Will Jacey's relationship with Asher invite the killer closer to her? Or is the killer already in her life?

"Screenplays: The Island Collection"
"Jungle Princess", "A.L.F. Resort", "Brighton Island"

Discover how romance and fun in the sun can be downright *chilling*!

"Jungle Princess" is a romantic/thriller that leaves a teenage girl stranded on an island with two male shipmates and a creature of "unknown" origin. She soon discovers the island is home to an abandoned prison with several prisoners roaming free. What really killed over one hundred prisoners? And is it still out there--?

"A.L.F. Resort" is a romantic/thriller set on an island resort with Artificial Life Forms as the main draw. At this resort, all your fantasies come true...until a malfunction removes safety inhibitors on the A.L.F.'s. Zombies, biker gangs, and mobsters run amuck, turning fantasies into nightmares. A young reporter gets more of a story than she anticipates, but will she survive long enough to write the story?

"Brighton Island" is a romantic/thriller set on a private island. When the owner's niece brings her psychic friend to the mansion, his presence awakens the spirits' tortured souls. As the psychic attempts to solve the old murders, the niece is confronted with the possibility that she's next to join the mansion ghosts. Stranded on the island with a crazed killer, her uncle wages his own war to save them. Will his "shock and awe" tactics actually save them or get them killed?

"Reaper of Souls"
A fantasy short story

A young woman must outwit an evil sorcerer in order to save her brother or become one of his minions forever.

Unwilling to believe her brother is dead, Reggie discovers an underhanded deal made with Kahn, a less than ethical sorcerer, who collects humans to serve as slaves in his kingdom. In order to rescue her brother from his horrible fate, she must complete his failed task or be forced to serve Kahn forever. After being transported to his world, Reggie realizes that even if she beats Kahn at his own game, she's at his mercy for him to uphold his end of the deal. All seems lost until Kahn's discontented, self-serving brother, Helsing, arrives. Can Reggie convince Helsing to help her? And at what cost?

"Death Displacement"

A grief-stricken man travels back in time to seek revenge on the woman who murdered his girlfriend but inadvertently falls in love with her.

Kane is about to marry the woman he loves. His life is perfect. A few weeks before the wedding, a vindictive woman from his girlfriend's past mysteriously arrives and kills her. He learns of a traumatic accident that happened five years earlier, which triggers Riley's hatred for his girlfriend. Distraught over his girlfriend's death, Kane uses an antique time machine to travel into the past in order to find and destroy the woman responsible. When he runs into Riley's younger self, he realizes she's not the monster she later becomes, and he can't bring himself to destroy her. With a little help from his oddball friend from the past, they formulate a plan to prevent the accident that sends Riley down her destructive path. Kane's plan backfires when he falls for the younger Riley. His new tortured existence is further complicated when future Riley, his girlfriend's killer, shows up with her own devious agenda that doesn't include him. Will he be able to stop the time ripple, which ultimately ends with his girlfriend's death? Or will future Riley take him out of the timeline forever--

"Dead Village"

After strange happenings isolate a small resort town from the rest of the world, nearly one hundred residents seek refuge at the closed hotel. Only eight survive the night. And that's just the beginning...

One day after the entire population of Fox Ridge Village disappears, a car wreck forces several unsuspecting crash victims to seek help at the closed summer hotel. Within the hotel, they discover the grisly aftermath of a brutal slaughter. Crash victims Vander and Devon, a reluctant clairvoyant, team up to solve the riddle of the "haunted hotel" and the mass hysteria plaguing the remaining survivors. By the time they discover the hotel's secret, they're already drawn into the hysteria. As the body count continues to climb, it's a race to isolate the source and bring everyone back to reality before they kill one another. Will Devon be able to communicate with the traumatized spirits before their fate becomes her own?

"Misfits, Inc."

A seemingly ordinary, young woman meets four misfits who claim she has given them supernatural powers.

While on a business trip to a remote island paradise, a bored secretary, Hailey, has her world turned upside down when her path collides with a psychic freak, Skyler. He attempts to convince her that they had met in his dreams, and she had chosen him as one of her four mystic warriors. After Skyler foresees a woman's death, they discover an unidentified creature has killed one of the guests. They are joined by a lounge pianist and a rich playboy, who also claim they had met her in their dreams. If Skyler's prophecies are genuine, the evil entity controlling the ravenous creatures needs to destroy Hailey to ensure its survival. Reluctantly accepting her fate, Hailey has to locate the last and most powerful of her chosen warriors, The Guardian. Their fate is in doubt when The Guardian turns out to be a self absorbed, former cat burglar with a bad attitude. Can Hailey turn her company of misfits into an elite team of mystic warriors? Or will The Guardian's secret agenda destroy them all?

"Basement Dwellers"

A viral outbreak at a hospital leaves a mortician, sheriff, and coroner fighting for their lives against a horde of undead and the CDC.

After a massive car wreck leaves several survivors in critical condition at the local hospital, a surgeon uses experimental drugs on his critical patients and accidentally causes a zombie outbreak. When local mortician, Lexx, receives an infected corpse as her client, she becomes stranded in the hospital basement during CDC quarantine along with the local sheriff and the coroner. The infamous surgeon struggles to find a cure for his infectious blunder by using the other survivors as test subjects. Meanwhile, Lexx and the sheriff attempt to locate his missing sister, who's stranded somewhere in the battle zone that once was the emergency room. It's a race against time and the ravenous undead. Can they survive the undead before CDC sanitizes the hospital of all infection?

"Witness Protection"
Also available in audiobook!

After witnessing an execution, a resourceful young woman attempts to disappear while being pursued by a hitman and a handsome federal agent.

A helicopter pilot, Jackie Remus, reluctantly agrees to go on a date with one of her clients, but her date is unexpectedly cut short when she witnesses a man being murdered. After narrowly escaping with her life, she is placed into protective custody. When the safe house is breached, Jackie makes a daring escape from both the hired killers and the handsome FBI agent, who wants to return her to protective custody. With a little help from her sly and crafty friend, Monroe, Jackie is convinced she can disappear until the trial. While on her journey to meet with her friend, she solicits help from a few shady but lovable characters along the way. Although she manages to stay one-step ahead of the hired killers, the federal agent remains in hot pursuit. Will Jackie reach Monroe before she's captured by the FBI and returned to protective custody? Or will the hired killers silence her first?

"Town Darling"

After surviving a brutal attack that claims the lives of those she loves, a young woman seeks revenge on a corrupt town.

Going back home is never easy, but for Casey, it means returning to her corrupt hometown where she barely survived a brutal attack. Accompanied by two family friends, she seeks justice for the night that destroyed her life. Her physical scars are nothing compared to her emotional ones, forcing the local sheriff to believe that the town darling is back for revenge. As the conspiracy for her revenge appears to be leading up to the coveted town fair, the sheriff is determined to stop her from fulfilling her vengeful scheme...but guilt over his role on that fateful night continues to haunt him. Will his desperate need for Casey's forgiveness be his undoing? Or will Casey's desire for revenge destroy them both?

"Unconditional"

A young woman puts her life on hold to care for an unstable, highly skilled combat soldier, who believes someone is trying to kill him.

A botched military coup leaves a team of elite fighters injured with one clinging to life in a coma. When Harlan wakes from his coma, he's left with no memory of his past life. His commander's daughter, Indy, takes it upon herself to care for the fallen war hero. She's challenged with more than just his physical care as she combats with not only his memory loss but also his newly found desire for her. His infatuation with her becomes the least of her worries when he sinks back into his role of a combat soldier. Believing his life is in danger, his fighting skills surface, turning him into an unpredictable and dangerous man. Will his memory return to him before Indy is forced to commit him? Or will he finally find his nemesis, "the coyote", and possibly claim the life of an innocent person?

"Witness Protection 2"
The Return of Whiskey Tango Foxtrot

Believing she holds the clue to millions in missing laundered money, a young woman is placed into the protective care of a former Navy SEAL team.

Feeling sorry for her recently separated co-worker, Leeann invites Wiley to join her and her friends on their night out. Little does she know that finding her co-worker murdered is just the beginning of her nightmare. Leeann unknowingly holds the key to fifty million dollars in potentially laundered mob money. With hired killers pursuing her, the FBI places her into a different kind of protective custody. Former Navy SEAL team Whiskey Tango Foxtrot reunites to keep Leeann alive at their secret hideaway. What should be an easy assignment takes an unscheduled turn when secrets, lies, and betrayal threaten to derail their mission. Is the team prepared for a war on their own doorstep? Will Leeann's misguided trust endanger the lives of those sent to protect her?

"Deadly Institution 2"

When blackmail turns into murder, a young woman finds herself caught in the killer's crosshairs.

The small town of Stony Ridge is no stranger to scandal and persecution of the innocent. When a brutal killing shakes the town's prestigious country club, Jacey McMurray seeks help from a self-proclaimed vigilante, Konrad Asher. As her professional and personal worlds collide, Jacey fears the stress of the country club killings have finally taken their toll on Asher. Can a stressed out vigilante stop the killer before he strikes again?

"Witness Protection 3"
Alpha Mike Foxtrot

A helicopter pilot risks her life to help a team of retired Navy SEALs rescue two girls from a killer.

When former Navy SEAL team Whiskey Tango Foxtrot asks for a simple favor, Jackie reluctantly offers her air-taxi services. What could go wrong? What begins as a search and rescue for two girls turns into a fight for survival against a heavily armed drug cartel. Wanted by the law with the cartel in hot pursuit and their home base breached, the team is forced to call in a favor from a questionable ally. Unfortunately, their new safe house isn't what it seems. Without knowing who the real enemy is, can Jackie and the team save their young witnesses from the hands of a killer?

Coming Soon!
"Witness Protection 4"

Holly Copella

ABOUT THE AUTHOR

Holly Copella has been writing since the age of twelve when her frustration at a book's poor plot drove her to author her own story. Over the last decade, she's written a number of screenplays, some of which she's now adapting into novels. Her fascination with zombies and other darker material lends an edge to her writing, which tends to lean toward horror. As a fan of Agatha Christie, she appreciates the craft of a good plot and the importance of creating significant characters.

Hailing from Pennsylvania, Copella lives in the Endless Mountains on a farm with her rescue horses and other animals. In addition to writing and reading fiction, she enjoys riding horses and traveling to Las Vegas and Disney World.